Broken Girls

Copyright © 2017 by J. M .R
Cover photo Stock Photo
Unsplash.com

All rights reserved. No part of this book may be reproduced or transmitted in any form without written permission from the publisher, except by a reviewer who may quote brief passages for review purposes. If you are reading this book and you have not purchased it or won it, this book has been pirated. Please delete the contents and purchase the book to from one of its distributors.

This is a work of fiction and any resemblance to any person, living or dead, any place, events or occurrences, is purely coincidental. The characters and story lines are created from the author's imagination or are used fictitiously.

Published by J. M. Ryan

Kendall,

I bow down to the awesomeness of your bookstagram. Hope you like this read. :)

Best,

J. M. Ryan

Dedication

Jenn, dreams don't come cheap. Thanks for the support and the fierce loyalty. This book wouldn't have seen the light of day without you. Gladiators forever.

Dad, I struggled with writing Candace's father so much, and it's because you are the best father in existence. Thanks for never failing me.

Chapter 1

My life as I knew it ended the day I discovered my father's affair. Sure, it would have been a terrible revelation no matter which way it shook out, but perhaps, had it been someone else he'd cheated with, my life wouldn't have imploded.

It was my senior year, and everything was coming up roses for me. Friends—check. Boyfriend—check. Future planned out—check. As I leaned back on a bulletin board and watched a girl try desperately to take down pictures stuck to the front of her locker, I believed I was untouchable.

The other students craned to look at the scandalous pictures, ones that would never be allowed in a school. The bulletin board supporting my weight was covered in anti-bullying ads; the irony wasn't lost on me.

"What do you think Vanessa's going to do when she realizes they're inside her locker too?" Mindy asked. Her red-lipstick smile was wide and menacing. Her dark hair contrasted against her pale skin. When she smiled genuinely, she looked like a pinup model. She was as beautiful as she was cruel. It gave me chills sometimes to watch her.

"Who cares?" Drea snorted. "She should have thought about that before she sent them to Allison's boyfriend." When a couple photos fell from the girl's hands, she laughed lightly and extended her bronzed legs out from her too-short white shorts even further in front of her. It took more self-assuredness to wear those, than I could ever dream to have, but that was Drea. She wore confidence like a second skin. "You dropped some," she called. Her caramel ponytail bounced slightly while she laughed.

Drea grew bored every now and then, and when she got bored, someone paid the price. Right now, Vanessa was the sacrificial lamb. There had been many others over the years, and we always bared witness.

Looking at the three girls around me, I wondered if I was the only one acting. I laughed with them as acid crawled up my throat.

For a while, no one moved forward to help Vanessa, but then a girl with hair like fire pushed through a few of onlookers and began grabbing photos. Shannon, a past sacrifice and the hardest to swallow. Even with her back to me, I knew it was her. There was a price for my popularity, and Shannon had paid it.

Vanessa's face was tomato red and tears streamed down as Shannon stuffed the photos in a bag. She wrapped her arm around Vanessa, and said something unintelligible.

"You satisfied?" Drea asked Allison.

Allison didn't seem to enjoy the show like the Mindy and Drea, but there was a victorious glint in her mousy face.

At Allison's nod, Drea picked up her purse. "Good, I'm bored." And she walked away without waiting to see if we would follow. We would. We always did.

I followed a bit quicker than I normally did. I wanted to be as far from the now-crying Vanessa and her companion as possible. I suspected Drea did too.

Drea led us to the bathroom on the second floor—deserted, as always. It was our pre-bell green room. It was our last chance to cover any imperfection. Every hair smoothed into place, makeup on point, and nails perfectly manicured. Sometimes when I looked in the mirror, I didn't recognize the girl looking back at me.

I emerged from the primping session, running a final hand through my blonde waves, when a pair of strong arms enveloped me. My ruby blouse rode up my stomach and a high-pitched squeal escaped me as the familiar warmth of Luke invaded my senses.

"Put me down!" I laughed.

"Good morning, beautiful," he whispered in my ear, making me shiver. He put me down and released me just long enough to turn me so my chest met his.

I wrapped my arms around his neck and played with the curls of blond hair that fell just over his collar. His hands dipped low and sank into the pockets of my tight blue jeans. He did this often, touched me in places that showed possession. It should have bothered me, but his emerald eyes made things hazy and his lips on mine made me forget to be angry at all. I was more than willing to be owned by him if it meant I could keep him.

"You two need a room," Drea called as she, Mindy, and Allison walked to first period.

"Maybe that's not such a bad idea." His breath fanned across my lips.

I slapped him lightly on the arm. "Keep dreaming. Walk me to first?"

"Want to come over after school?" Luke kissed my fingers as we stopped outside my first period class. The wisps of hair on his chin tickled my hand.

"I can't. Drea and I are having a girls' night."

"Ah yes, your other significant other," Luke teased, although there was a hardness in his eyes.

"How about tomorrow?" I asked, trying to bring back his adoring gaze.

"Maybe. I might be busy." He stuck his lower lip out to pout.

I stood up on my toes and kissed him. "Well, maybe I'll make it worth your while."

His face cleared and he cupped my face to give me a quick, hard kiss. "I'll text you later."

I watched him walk down the hallway. He looked so good in those jeans.

After school, Drea and I spent a couple of hours trying on clothes at a new boutique just outside of Brinkerville. If you wanted any fashionable clothing, buying them inside of Brinkerville, NH wasn't an option. We had a used clothing store, and that was pretty much it. Drea wasn't about to set foot in there, which meant I wasn't either.

The drive there and back gave us more time to be just the two of us. When we were alone, without Mindy and Allison, it was always easier to relax. Drea seemed less on edge, and she laughed a lot more—not the cruel kind of laughter, either. She'd been nicknamed Dreaded Drea, I wasn't sure by whom, our freshmen year. People never said it to her face, but it could be heard in the hushed whispers of those who feared her, which was pretty much everyone.

"Still want to hit the movies?" Drea asked as we put shopping bags in the back of her car. The smooth black interior still smelled new. It was hard not to feel envious every time I got into it. I drove mom's five-year-old Corolla most of the time.

"I'm kinda beat. What if we just watched one on Netflix instead?" It was supposed to be a girls' night, but I just didn't have it in me to stay out. Yoga pants were calling my name.

"You want to stay over?" she asked sympathetically. She took her eyes off the road momentarily to give me an understanding glance.

"Yeah, that'd be great."

Drea was the only one I'd told about my parents and their nightly arguments. They had been worse recently and ended mostly with my father sleeping in the guest room.

Looking back, there had been signs my parents weren't happy, but somehow I'd missed them. Perhaps I'd simply been too close. Too close to pay much attention to how we rarely did anything together as a family. Dad took me to the movies and my mother cried "headache." My mother taught me how to cook family recipes while my father worked later and later every night. Yeah, the signs were there, but I still didn't see the end coming until it hit me right in the fucking face.

When Drea pulled into her driveway, I was surprised to see the familiar SUV in front of her house.

"Isn't that your dad's car?" Drea asked as she released her seatbelt.

I nodded in confusion. That morning my father had told my mother and me that he would be out of town for a meeting all day. Had something bad happened?

I took my phone out to see if I'd any missed calls from either of my parents, but there were none. "Maybe my parents want me home or something," I said, unsure.

Drea and I collected our bags from the back of her car and made our way inside. There was no one in the front study and kitchen—all we found were a pair of empty wine glasses.

Drea halted momentarily as she took in the wine glasses and then sped up her searching. I followed her as she made her way to the back living room. When she eased the doors open, I nearly collided into the back of her.

"Jesus, Drea," I murmured, as I sidestepped her frozen stature.

The room was messier than normal. Clothes were scattered about. My blood ran cold at the sight of them. White-hot rage blazed a trail through my veins and spread throughout my body. My father and Drea's mother, May…

"What the fuck?" Drea cried, but still didn't move. Her body was hard as marble beside me.

At the sound of her voice my father sprung off of May and promptly tripped over the metal coffee table with a grunt of pain. As he righted himself, his face drained of color. Clumsily, he covered his naked torso as May sat up with a pillow clutched to her chest.

"Shit, shit," my father whispered, as he raked his hands over his face.

I tried not to dry heave, focusing instead on the flower pattern wallpaper. I'd stared at it many times while sitting on the couch that I would never, ever sit on again.

"Drea, honey, it's not what it looks like," May said, scrambling to find her shirt.

"I'm not really sure what else it could be," Drea choked out. The anger coming from her was palpable, and I thought if I touched her, my fingertips would burn and blister.

I stood wanting numbness to take me, but it didn't come. I felt every bit of rage and confusion. This wasn't my life. It couldn't be. My father, the man I depended on, could not be a cheater.

May found her shirt and quickly buttoned it. Once it was in place, she turned to me. "Oh Candace!" she cried and took a step toward me, but I held my hands up to ward her off.

"You missed one," I said and pointed to the lowest button.

May's hands slapped the place I indicated. She turned to my father and touched his arm. "Walt, you should go. I want to talk to Drea alone."

My eyes locked onto May's hand on dad's arm. Her French tips light on his skin. It was somehow much more personal, more intimate than how we'd first caught them. There were feelings between them, I realized. Whatever we'd just walked in on, it wasn't a simple mistake.

My father hesitated, as if he didn't know how to say goodbye to her with us standing here. My stomach lurched.

After a moment, he shook his head slightly and walked over to me. He tried to put his hand on my shoulder to guide me out, but I brushed him off violently. I smelled May's perfume on him.

"I can walk myself," I spat.

Dad's brows furrowed in hurt.

As I left, I reached out for Drea, but her head whipped toward me, and the hate in her gray eyes was sharp enough to make me pause. I tried to tell her I would text her later, but the words stuck in my throat.

Dad was silent as we walked to the car, but words began to flow from him as he got into the driver's seat beside me. Excuses and apologies poured from his mouth, but static filled my ears. He was a liar. How could I believe anything he said? The image of May and dad entwined was all I saw as he spoke. Did he think of her when he was with Mom and me?

Mom. Glancing at the time displayed on the dashboard, I knew she would be home when we arrived. She was probably going about her day like it was any other, oblivious to the wrecking ball driving her way.

"Candace? Are you listening to me?" my father said. His eyes shot over to me every few seconds.

"How could you do this to mom?"

Dad was silent. "I know. I know it's not right. I… I love her."

For the first time since the death of my brother, my father began to cry. At my brother's funeral, I'd held my father's hand and offered him strength. I refused to do that now.

"Then why would you do this to her?" My vision blurred with rage. I couldn't help but think of Luke. How many times had he cheated? How many times had he used the word *love* to win me back?

My father shook with emotion next to me, but I turned my head toward the window. I tried to count trees to distract myself. It was August, but the trees were still bare in some places—as if the leaves were already dying again.

We rode the remainder of the way in silence, tension thick in the air. By the end of the drive, I could barely breathe.

I didn't wait for my father while he parked the car. Instead, I sprinted to find my mother, praying somehow that I could save her from the hurt hurtling toward her. Taking the porch steps two at a time, I ignored dad's plea for me to wait.

Mom was carrying a laundry basket down the stairs when I slammed the front door behind me. Her face broke into a smile, but it flattened when she took me in.

Tears started to roll down my face.

She dropped the laundry basket and engulfed me in her arms, making little sounds as she rubbed my back, like she had done when I was little.

My back tensed with the clicking of the front door.

"What the hell is going on, Walt? What is all this?" Mom kept her arms around me, but she stared directly at my father.

"Candace, can you give us some time to talk, please." He stood in front of the front door. Pictures of our life together decorated the walls beside him.

I held my mother tighter with no intention of letting her go. He may not know much about loyalty, but I did.

"Candace, please," he whispered. His eyes pleaded with me, but I wasn't moved.

My mother slowly disentangled my arms from around her body. My mascara had stained the right shoulder of her shirt. "Candace, give us a moment," she said. When I opened my mouth to argue, she held up her hand. "It'll be okay. Head upstairs."

She was wrong; nothing was ever going to be okay again. Reluctantly, I made my way up the stairs, stopping when I was just out of eyesight. I kept my movements and breath light. She might have sent me away, but I was going to be ready if she needed me.

"What is going on here? She came in looking like someone had died. Oh, God! Did something happen to Drea?" My mother's voice was muffled slightly by the distance, but her worry rang through.

"No, no one is hurt…She just saw something. Something I—I never meant for her to see."

"What do you mean she saw something?" I could picture her crossing her arms just as she did when I gave vague answers about what kept me out so late some nights.

"Maybe we should sit down," Dad said lowly.

The next moments of silence were broken only by the sound of slow footsteps. I waited for a few moments, but found, much to my frustration, that they had moved too far for me to hear. I crept silently down the stairs, careful to avoid the middle stair that always creaked, and held my breath. I was almost to the bottom stair when their voices became audible again.

"I'm sorry, Cindy. I didn't mean for this," Dad said, sounding tired. "I know there's not much I can say to make this easier." My father's voice was steady, far steadier than it had been in the car.

"We made promises, Walt. We promised to stick it out." I couldn't see her, but I had a horrible image in my mind of her sitting in one our wooden kitchen chairs, folding into herself as if she could physically stop him from destroying the life they'd built.

"I know. I'm sorry. I'm so, so sorry," his voice cracked. "I love her."

My mother's sniffling and fast breathing were almost enough for me to go to her, but I found myself collapsing instead. Numbness, the kind I'd wanted so badly when I'd first seen my father and May, took me over. Pins and needles radiated through my body, spreading to my every limb. I understood now that I had misunderstood him in the car. It wasn't my mother he loved.

After a few moments, my mother lobbed him with questions of how long it had gone on and what happens next, but in the days that followed I wouldn't be able to recall what his answers were. It was as if I was outside of my own body, watching the events of my life play out rather than living them.

When I couldn't take anymore of my father's truth, I left the stairs and went to my room. Part of me wished I had stayed here the whole time. Maybe then, my hatred for my father would be less. I didn't know how long I sat at my desk, waiting for whatever came next. A few tears escaped as I looked at a family picture from just a few years prior. It was from before my brother's accident. We'd been on our family ski trip and had asked a man to take our picture at the lodge. We were all smiles. We were happy.

"I wish you were here," I whispered to the picture. My brother would have known what to do. He would have held us all together.

My father appeared at my door less than an hour later with a suitcase in hand, and I knew then: we were really and truly finished. He was leaving my mother, and he was leaving me.

"I'm going to the hotel for the night." His grip on his suitcase was tight, his knuckles white .

"And after tonight?" I asked quietly.

"I'm not sure, to be honest. Your mother and I have a bit to figure out. You're going to stay with her for the time being," he said robotically. He'd practiced it before getting to my door, I was sure.

"You can't just abandon us," I said and hated how it sounded like I was begging him, which in a way, I was.

He sighed. For a moment it looked like he was going to come into my room, but he seemed to think better of it. "Your mother and I…it's complicated, Candace."

"There's nothing complicated about not cheating on your wife."

Dad blanched. "When you're calm, we can discuss this further. I never wanted to hurt you."

"Austin would hate you for this," I said levelly.

My father reared back as if I'd slapped him. I'd never used Austin's memory like that before. I wanted to reach into the space between the two of us, grab the words and force them back down my throat.

My father's lips tightened. "I know," he whispered, and he left.

I waited until I heard his car engine start before I allowed myself to crumble. I curled on my bed and cried for my mother, my life, even Drea. Her life, too, had been blown apart. I wasn't sure at what point in the night my mother came in, but when I woke the next morning, her arms were wrapped around me.

In her sleep, she looked vulnerable in a way that scared me. I wrapped my arms tightly around her and when she woke, we both cried.

"What are we going to do?" I asked, tasting salted tears and sorrow.

"Survive," my mother said. Her voice was missing something, but there was resolve in her eyes. We would survive. A deserter would not break the Ellis women.

Chapter 2

I stayed out of school the remainder of the week. Mom called me out sick, and my teachers emailed my homework.

Mom only missed one day of work and she shed no tears as she packed dad's things. I, on the other hand, wasn't as strong. I still cried in my bed at night, silently, so she would never know.

I sent Drea a couple of texts, but the only person who ever reached out was my father. His voicemails and texts were always the same: apologetic and insufficient.

Luke came by some nights, but I didn't tell him the whole truth. Just that my dad left.

I switched out sweatpants for leggings toward the end of the week, so mom would stop giving me looks of concern every time she came home from work to find me exactly where she'd left me that morning.

I didn't ask mom much about her plan moving forward, but she did mention the petition for divorce that dad would be served. I didn't know what it meant for us or what the consequences would be. She thought she was protecting me from not saying much about her conversations with him, I knew, but it felt like I wandering through this blind.

I was surprised when she finally brought him up over dinner at the end of the week.

"Your father and I spoke today," she said, gauging my reaction.

I tried to keep my face impassive as I said, "Oh yeah?"

Mom nodded. Her lips thinned a bit before she spoke. "We're trying to keep everything civil. Unfortunately, we've hit a bit of a snag."

"What kind of snag?"

"He has some conditions." After a brief pause, she said lowly, "He is willing to give us the house and other funds if you agree to dinner with him once a week."

I sputtered at the suggestion, almost knocking my glass over.

My mother held up her hands. "Candace, I didn't tell you to put pressure on you. I told you so I wouldn't be making decisions for you when it comes to your father. It's your call whether or not you want a relationship with him."

A different, even more unsettling thought crept in. "If I said no, would we be okay? Like with the house and everything?"

"Of course we would. I don't want you to worry about things like that. I'll call your father and tell him no." She sent me a tight smile, and I got the feeling we wouldn't be as okay as she wanted me to believe.

Later, when I was sure she was asleep, I dialed his number for the first time since he'd left. He answered on the second ring, almost as if he were waiting for me. It wasn't a long conversation; it took only minutes to discuss the logistics. I would attend dinner, and he would give mom whatever she wanted and needed. It was a contract, not a relationship.

On Saturday morning, Mindy texted me about her party. Luke had mentioned it in passing, but he was going away with his family, so he didn't plan on going. At first I wasn't sure, but when Mindy begged, I relented. Luke wouldn't love that I was going without him, but he'd get over it. Besides, it was my chance to see Drea. We were the only two who knew what the other was going through.

"Where is she?" I asked Mindy over the music.

"She said she was hanging out with her dad or something," Mindy said coolly. In fact, she had been rather chilly to me all night. I wasn't sure how much Drea had told her and Allison about our parents, so I kept my mouth shut.

I hung around the party for a few hours, hoping maybe Drea would show. To my disappointment, however, Drea never did.

Mindy and Allison stuck together all night, making me feel like the third wheel. The vibe between the three of us was way off. I felt like they were assessing me in a way they never had before. Like I was prey.

Instead of making awkward conversation with either of them, I spent the night getting drunk, and Mindy's brother had to drive me home. It wasn't my finest hour, and I threatened to break his hand if he tried to touch my ass again. The night was pointless, and the only thing I got out of it was a killer headache the next day.

***

I pulled into the school parking lot on Monday determined to carry on as normal. I spotted Drea sitting on a bench with Mindy and Allison the moment I entered the front quad. People gave them a wide berth, but they stood just close enough to answer the call should Drea want to pull them into her inner circle.

I felt a sense of relief at the sight of her. She looked the same, maybe a little paler, but the same, and *we* would be the same. We would fix whatever was wrong between us. We would be okay.

"Hey Drea," I said and sat down on the bench, taking care to tuck my skirt under me.

For a moment, none of them moved. My neck prickled when Mindy and Allison scowled at me, and Drea wrinkled her nose like she smelled something disgusting.

"Can we help you?" Mindy growled. She uncrossed her legs like she was ready to lunge if Drea gave the order.

I straightened up, confused, but readying myself. "What's going on?"

"As if you don't know." Allison rolled her eyes.

"Actually, I don't." None of this was right. This wasn't how it was supposed to go.

I laid my hand on Drea's arm, but she ripped her arm out of my grasp. "Don't touch me," Drea said, as she rubbed where I'd touched.

"What the hell, Drea?" I pulled my hands into my lap. Looking around, I saw onlookers giving us curious glances. It was the first time since middle school that I felt uncomfortable under their gaze.

"What did you think would happen?" Drea whispered. "Did you think that we'd still be besties after your dad screwed my mom?" The look on Drea's face was menacing and hateful. I'd seen it before, but never directed at me.

Her words vibrated through my body, ricocheting off my bones. "My dad wasn't the only one doing the screwing," I said, fighting the urge to wipe away the sweat that had broken out over my hairline.

"What's so wrong with your mother that he had to prey on another woman?"

Anger boiled in me. If Drea wanted to insult my mother, I could fight like that too. "Maybe if your mother wasn't such a whore, none of this would have happened," I shot back.

Mindy and Allison's sharp intakes of breath were the only audible sounds as Drea's hands sprung out quickly and caught me in the chest. I only had a moment to register the air going out of my lungs before Drea shoved me again, and I tumbled from the bench onto the hard blacktop below. Pain reverberated up from my tailbone and arms where I had tried to catch myself.

I pushed onto my elbows and looked up to see my three former friends towering over me.

Drea bent down closer to my face, so the smell of her spearmint toothpaste wafted into my nose. "You're a fucking bitch. You were nothing before me and now you're going to be less than that. I'm going to ruin you. When I'm done, you'll be a fucking pariah." She stood up and brought a hand to her hair to make sure it was in place.

The three turned and walked toward the school, skirts swishing behind them.

I eased myself into a standing position and gave myself the once over. My blouse was torn slightly, and I had scrapes on my elbows. Overall, it stung, but it could have been worse. I tried to ignore the eyes on me as I brushed my back off. None of them had even tried to help me.

"It's one thing for you to try to take over my life and hurt me," Drea shouted and paused for a moment. I knew she was making sure she had the attention of the quad. She stood just before the entrance of the school, so she was in the middle of everything. "But to betray Luke like that is way over the line."

At the mention of Luke's name, fear spiraled in my chest. The crowd of people stared at me with accusations in their eyes.

Drea smirked at me one last time and disappeared into the school.

As I made my way through the crowd, I could hear them whispering my name. I sped up my pace, surprised I didn't leave skid marks on the linoleum as I searched for Luke. He wasn't waiting for me in any of our usual spots, and with every passing moment, the pit in my stomach expanded.

I barely paid attention to my classes all morning. It would be a pain to try and teach myself the lessons later, but all I could think about was finding Luke. Drea's words kept replaying in my head. *To betray Luke like that*. I'd never betrayed Luke, not once.

Finally I found him, walking in the hallway before lunch. My heart leapt into my throat when I finally spotted him. I knew it was bad right away. He looked defeated—shoulders slumped, head down. Luke Jackson never looked defeated.

He didn't look up and see me until he almost reached his locker. His mouth tightened more and more with each step he took. He opened his locker to change out books without saying a word to me.

Luke had never given me the silent treatment before. Even when he had been in one of his jealous rages, he still spoke to me. He kept his eyes focused on his books.

"Luke," I said softly. I wanted so badly to touch him, to cup his face and make him look at me.

He slammed his locker shut and shoved his phone into my hands. Confusion ran through me. I wanted to laugh and vomit at the same time.

It was a photo of Mindy's brother and me from the night of the party. I'd been drunk that night, but I'd had enough of my wits to shove Mindy's brother off when he'd tried to kiss me. This picture had been taken right before that moment. Someone had to have waited for the exact right moment to take that picture.

Who would sink that low? Within seconds, I knew. Drea. I knew Drea enough to recognize her handiwork. Mindy's plea for me to attend the party made perfect sense now.

"That isn't what it looks like," I stammered.

He took the phone from my hands and shoved it into his back pocket. Disgust filled his face. I could soften him; he was still the boy I loved. I could fix this—I knew I could. I reached out to touch his face, and for a moment, he let me. He turned his cheek into my hand and closed his eyes. But right when I believed we were going to be okay, he pushed my hand aside.

"You sure that's what you want to go with?" His tone was low and cold. It surprised me enough to make me take a step back.

"I'm telling you the truth. That isn't what it looks like."

He started to turn away from me, but I grabbed his arm and stepped around him to block his way. "Ask Mindy's brother, Adam. He'll tell you that nothing happened. He tried to kiss me, and I rejected him. I didn't tell you because I knew you'd be jealous."

"Don't you think I already did that?" He grabbed my hand roughly to remove it from his arm. "I called him after that photo was sent to me." He went back to staring at the ground. His jaw worked back and forth.

"So why are you so mad at me? I don't get it!" He couldn't be mad at me for someone else's actions. I should have told him about Adam, but he got so… so mad sometimes.

"Adam told me that you said you were single and that you two hooked up." His voice dipped low on the last part.

"He didn't really say that," I whispered. Adam had lied. How could he have lied?

"As if that weren't enough, a lot of people saw you leave the party with him." He slammed his fist against the locker.

A few people walking by stopped and stared.

I shook my head. "He was the sober driver. I didn't leave *with* him. He just drove me home. Luke, please, you have to believe me. Nothing happened. I wouldn't… I love you. I would never do that." I fought back tears and reached for him again, but he sidestepped me.

"The proof is right here, in the photo. You made me look like an *idiot*, Candace. Everyone knows about this. You think I can just ignore it and stay with you? This is humiliating."

"Are you kidding?" I said. "How do you think it felt all the times you cheated on me?"

"Is that why you did this? No… don't answer that. I don't care. You made your bed. Lie in it." He shook his head and walked away, like he couldn't stand to be near me for another second.

The one or two people in the hallway didn't even pretend to look away. I walked in the opposite direction Luke had gone, wandering until I found an empty classroom to hide in. I sat down and cried until my eyes burned and my chest hurt. Everyone I counted on had been ripped from me: Drea, my father, Luke. How could I have been so wrong about the people I believed in?

Drea. I had given up so much for her. Pieces of myself. While I'd spent the week missing her, she'd spent it planning my downfall.

True to her word, she had made me a social pariah. Enemy number one. Luke was the star of the basketball team, the homecoming king, the golden boy of Brinkerville High School. And now, thanks to Drea, everyone believed I was the slut who betrayed him and broke his heart.

CHAPTER 3

Two Months Later

Whore.

The word was painted in black on the outside of my locker. I barely gave it a second glance as I twisted my combination lock. I was more concerned with the interior, but they left it alone this time; although it still smelled a bit like the deli meat someone had left to rot over Columbus Day weekend. That had been lovely to come back to. They'd spelled *whore* right this time, which I guess earned them points, but they were getting less and less creative if they had to revert to old material.

I heard whispers and felt eyes boring down on my back, but I played it casual until I heard a piercing, shrill laugh.

"Candace, so glad you're finally owning who you are," Drea said, with a whip of her caramel hair. "And displaying it for the whole school to see, so brave."

Standing before her, I felt like I always did now: small and grungy. Drea looked flawless. Each strand of her hair was curled to perfection, and her romper was perfectly in place. To most people she looked utterly casual, but I knew she'd laid out that outfit last night and compared it with at least three others. After all, who had taught me to do the same thing, not that I bothered to take the time anymore?

Mindy and Allison flanked Drea, both looking effortlessly beautiful, but careful at the same time to not outshine their commander. They wore identical smiles, the ones without teeth, like they were ready to turn them into snarls if the moment presented itself. Deep down, I knew I had once looked the same way.

"Is this getting old for you yet, Drea?" I sighed and tried not to notice how many people stopped around us.

Drea cocked her head to the side and smirked. "Not even close. Why? Are you close to breaking?" She opened her mouth to go on, but she must have felt the air change the only way it can in high school when a teacher approaches.

"Me?" Drea said, loud enough for Mr. Chagnon to hear. She raised her hand to her chest dramatically. "Honestly Candace, we used to be friends. How could you think I would do something like this to you? I'm hurt, really."

I rolled my eyes. *And the award goes to...*

But Mr. Chagnon didn't look like he bought Drea's act. He seemed to be looking to me for signs that Drea was lying through her teeth, but I stayed silent. I knew Drea too well. I knew that she would turn up the torture if I said anything. I wasn't about to make an amateur mistake like that.

When I said nothing, Mr. Chagnon sent everyone on their way, but ordered me to stick around. Drea shot a warning glare over her shoulder as she disappeared into the crowd, her hair dancing behind her.

"This is the third time in a handful of months someone has decided to decorate your locker, Miss Ellis. You ready to talk yet?" He sent me a small smile, in what I assumed was an attempt to lure me into a sense of ease, but I wasn't ready to talk. I would never be, but I couldn't say that to him, so instead I let my eyes fall to the floor.

"I can't help you if you don't talk. If I don't see them do it, I can't take action." To his credit, he and his shiny, bald head genuinely looked like he wanted to help me.

"Mr. Chagnon, if I knew, I'd tell you, but I don't. Some struggling artist is just obsessed with me or so something," I said, trying to make light of it.

He looked unsure, but he didn't call me back when I made my way toward first period. As if my morning hadn't started off rocky enough, Chemistry was my first period class.

I arrived late and earned a warning glance from Mr. Mason, the usually smiley Chemistry teacher. No one said anything as I passed by, but almost all of them stared. All of them except for Shannon and her lab partner, Mark. Instead, they sat at their lab table in back and talked quietly. Seeing their closeness sent a jolt of longing through me.

I'd never given much thought about popularity before Drea. I'd never cared if people looked at me oddly for loving *Pokémon* or *Harry Potter*. Nerds were normally eaten alive in middle school, but I'd found a kindred soul in Shannon. She'd told me once, "If you really think you're a Gryffindor, I'll be a Hufflepuff. Everybody needs a Hufflepuff friend. Hufflepuffs keep friend groups grounded."

Shannon had moved to my cul-de-sac in Brinkerville the summer before Kindergarten. It had been the same year I'd asked my parents for a sister who was my age. Turned out I'd gotten a form of my wish when the moving trucks had rolled in.

I was so focused on Shannon that I hadn't heard Mr. Mason tell us to start the labs. It was only when Mindy saddled up to my table that I realized I had missed something.

"Ready, partner?" she crooned. To anyone who didn't know her, they would think she was being pleasant, but I knew it was going to be a rough class. Especially since she wasted no time digging her black-painted nails into my arm as she spoke.

It didn't take long for Mindy to spill the liquids we were working on all over me, which caused Mr. Mason to rush me to washing station. It was only ink, but I would wear the mark of Mindy's hatred around all day. She sent me a smug smile as she left the room, and I was left to clean up the best I could. It was only late October. How was I going to survive the rest of the year like this?

***

Fridays were usually my longest days during the week. Not only did I have school, but I also had work. Working at the movie theater wasn't my dream job, but hey, I took what I could get.

"Candy!" Joe exclaimed. "Not only on time, but five minutes early. Is hell freezing over?" His eyes blinked with false curiosity as he leaned around me to see outside, like he was actually concerned for the state of the world. He was fresh sometimes, but it was endearing.

Joe had worked at the theater too long for his own good, but he was the only friend I had at the moment. At twenty-one, Joe was blessed to have been old enough to graduate before Drea's reign of terror at Brinkerville High. And it was lucky, because if he had, he would have most likely despised me like the rest of the movie theater staff.

No matter what they did, Drea would have the high-school aged movie theater staffers redo it whenever she came in.

"Too much butter."

"Not enough salt."

"I said Sour Patch Kids, not Gummy Bears."

And as we walked into the designated theater, Drea would comment on the looks of the workers or how desperate they must have been to work there with just enough volume for everyone to hear. I, being a sheep, had laughed right along with Mindy and Allison.

Maybe in the end that was why I decided the theater was just the place to work. I felt an odd satisfaction in aligning with the people Drea believed to be beneath her, even if said people didn't exactly care for me.

"My name's not Candy. I know you struggle with learning new things, but you can master this. I've got faith," I said sweetly. "Besides, I got here early just because I couldn't wait to see your face."

"Believe me, the rest of us could have waited to see yours," Rachel muttered, coming out of the break room. Her black hair was tied in a tight pony tale and her blue eyes barely glanced at me as she lobbed her insult.

Rachel reserved a special kind of hatred for me, as she had once been the unfortunate victim of my jealousy.

Sophomore year, Luke had started having trouble in History. Rachel, who had been exceptionally quiet and mousy, had been the girl he'd chosen to study with. It had been impossible to miss the way Rachel's eyes would widen every time he approached, but when she'd flirted with him right in front of me, she'd crossed a line. I'd made the choice to vent to Drea, knowing full well what I was doing.

It had taken only a day for the rumor that Rachel was a lesbian to spread around school, and by the end of the day, someone had carved *DYKE* into her locker.

I still had that look seared into my memory, the one on Rachel's face when she found her defaced locker. I still remember the look she had shot us when Drea and I had cackled at her. The girl had gone from just a face in the crowd to everyone knowing her as the only lesbian at Brinkerville High in two seconds flat.

I avoided Rachel the best I could whenever we worked the same shift. I wasn't foolish enough to think she would ever forgive me. But even if I were, Rachel made it abundantly clear that she had no forgiveness in her heart.

She'd been the one to train me on my first day at the movie theater, and it quickly became obvious her goal was to either make me quit or get me fired. She'd tricked me into giving customers free candy. "It's promotional," she'd said. And then there had been the toilet cleaner incident. I'd found out from my extremely ticked-off boss that employees never, ever gave away any products, and the cleaner used on the soda fountains was in the orange bottles, not the white. In other words, toilet cleaner was not for use on the soda fountains.

Somehow I got to keep my job, but I did have to convince myself to go back for my second shift. Surprisingly, when I had walked up to Rachel ready for another night of hell, she'd avoided me, and Joe had stepped in.

I later found out Joe had taken up for me, and while I hadn't asked him why at first, I'd eventually let my curiosity get the better of me. I'd asked him if he Rachel had told him about our history, and when he avoided eye contact and let out a breath, I knew Rachel had told him everything.

"You decided to help me anyway?"

He'd nodded. "You bullied her. She bullied you. It's not a cycle I want to see continue. Besides, you getting a job here instead of just coming in to make our lives miserable with your bitchy friend tells me you're probably in a rough spot."

"You remembered me, and you decided to still be nice to me?" I'd tried to think about the last time someone had been kind to me, but hadn't been able to.

"I'd love to tell you that I've been nice like this my whole life, but the truth is I've done enough shit to feel guilty for. Kicking you when you're already down isn't something I care to be a part of, even if you did some really shitty things to Rachel."

I'd almost said Rachel wasn't nearly the only one I'd tormented, but decided it wouldn't help my case. "You're a better person than most people I know." It was a kindness I hadn't deserved, but one I was eternally grateful for.

"You must only have met the world's shittiest people," he'd said teasingly, but I'd detected the slightest bit of pity mixed in.

Fridays at the movie theater were always busy, and since I didn't have much of a social life, I volunteered to work almost all of them. Brinkerville was small enough to be boring. There were a few shops downtown, but most people went outside Brinkerville for entertainment. Seeing movies was a way to kill time, and it became a regular thing to have kids I went to high school with hop in my line so they could laugh at me as I waited on them. Generally, I ignored their stares. That was probably why I didn't realize Shannon was in my line until I looked up and met a familiar pair of brown eyes, just a shade lighter than my own.

"Hey," I said, forgetting for a moment to open with the "What can I get for you today" line all employees had drilled into our heads.

"I'll take a small popcorn and a job application," she said curtly. Her red hair was pulled back into a neat braid; it stretched her face, so her eyes looked even bigger.

"I thought your dad always said you weren't allowed to get a job." The words slipped from me, dipping back into the memories of our friendship. When we had been young, we'd talked about getting jobs the moment we were old enough, mostly so we could buy phones to communicate instead of the walkie-talkies we had. Shannon's father had overheard the conversation and wasted no time telling Shannon her focus would be on school and family, and there would be no time for jobs.

"It's not for me," she said forcefully and pursed her lips. I suspected her mind had gone to the same memory, or maybe I just hoped.

Behind Shannon, there was a bit of awkward laughter. A few members of the Top Ten stood behind her.

On the first day of tenth grade, a new Shannon had emerged. Gone were the graphic t-shirts and baggy jeans. She seemed determined to be the best and the smartest and she fell in quickly with others of the same mindset. Almost immediately, Drea nicknamed them the "Top Ten," playing off of the high-school tradition to publish the senior pictures of the top ten students in the graduating class in the newspaper.

The nickname wasn't super clever, especially since not all of the top ten students actually hung out together, but no one had dared to say that to Drea.

Now they stood before me with neutral faces that bordered on dislike. Mark's face held the most open hostility. Even though his eyes and hair were dark, almost black, the dark expression didn't look right on him.

"It's for me," Mark said and raised his hand. His dark eyes surveyed me. It was clear he felt the same about me as everyone else did.

"You want to work here?"

"The diner isn't hiring, so I'm not really left with a whole lot of local options. If your boss asks, yes I want to work here more than anything." This got a laugh from of few of the other Top Ten members.

"Is there a reason this line isn't moving?" Robby, the shift manager, asked quietly behind me. His black suit that fit too tightly over his stomach rubbed against me inadvertently.

I moved to grab the popcorn and job application. "Just trying to find our job applications," I said innocently.

As I handed over everything to Shannon and Mark and watched them walk away with their friends, I felt a feeling like sorrow blaze through me.

"You okay? You look like you saw a ghost," Joe said, giving me a slight nudge with his shoulder.

A dark laugh came from behind us, and we both turned to see Rachel stuffing a bag of popcorn. She met my eyes purposefully before looking at Joe. "She almost *was* a ghost because of Candace."

Joe looked at me, but I pretended not to feel his curious gaze as I turned to help the next customer in line. *A Ghost*. Perhaps that was why I had always felt haunted by her.

***

The following morning, Dad texted me to set up our weekly dinner date. Just a few days later, I found him sitting at a table in the center of the restaurant. He was in his usual suit, and I, as usual, was underdressed for the venue. At our first dinner, he'd hinted to me that my outfit of leggings and a hoodie wasn't entirely appropriate; now I wore too causal clothing just to annoy him.

"Candace, how was school?" he asked, looking at his watch to see how late I was.

I shrugged, non-committedly; I had purposefully taken my time getting here, as I did every week. I wouldn't be here if I didn't have to be, and I had decided I would subtly, or not so subtly, let him know it.

"It's almost time for college applications to go out. Have you been working on them?"

Again, I found a way to answer without speaking. This time I sent him a nod and pretended to look at the menu. The food here was too fancy, but I was still bitter enough to order the most expensive thing on the menu, not that he would notice.

"That's good. Is Dartmouth still your top choice?"

Another nod. I busied myself by buttering a roll and stuffing it into my mouth.

"Your mother tells me you're working a lot to pay for it. College is terribly expensive these days. Even if you don't get into Dartmouth, the loans will be vicious." He sipped his wine.

My chewing slowed. There was something in his tone that made me look at him against my wishes.

He smiled when he saw he had my full attention. "Your mother also tells me that your aunt Susan is coming to stay with you while your mother goes on her business trip next week."

I placed the remainder of my roll on my bread plate. Curiosity had gotten the better of me. He was going somewhere with this, and I had a feeling I would hate it. "Yeah, so?"

"Well, there's really no reason for Susan to have to come down here when there are plenty of extra rooms at my house."

I stared at him like he'd lost his mind. "You're delusional."

He smiled like I'd made a joke. "Actually, quite the opposite," he said. "I'm prepared to offer you a deal. I'll cover Dartmouth, or whatever college you decide, if you stay with me for the few months your mother is away."

In that moment, I was exceptionally lucky there were only butter knives on the table because I was sure I would have thrown a sharper one at him if I'd had it. He *knew* what Dartmouth meant to me. How hard I had worked. He also knew I would do just about anything to keep my mother out of debt, which she would very surely go into trying to help me pay for it.

"Do you really think living together will make any of this"—I indicated to both of us—"any better? You think manipulating me into this is really the right move?"

"Unfortunately, you've left me with few options. You come to dinner and barely speak to me, you refuse to take any olive branch I try to extend, so yes, in this circumstance I do believe it's the right move."

I glared at him until I thought I would cry. "You can't buy my love back."

"No," he said sadly, "but I can buy your time. With it, maybe you'll forgive me."

I lowered my eyes, hating him more passionately than I ever could have imagined possible. How was this the same man I had ever once adored?

He sighed. "All you have to do is stay with me Candace and just try. That's all. I'll give you whatever you want if you just try."

I didn't look at or speak to him for the remainder of dinner. We both knew what my decision would be. I hated him for backing me into a corner, and I hated myself for letting him.

CHAPTER 4

Everyone had always said high school would be so different. So new. What I hadn't realized until my first day of ninth grade was that I could be new too.

It had been mom's idea to ditch my *Star Wars* shirt and baggy jeans. I'd never been so uncomfortable getting out of a car as I was that morning, and I'd broken my foot in the third grade. Crutches were nothing compared to skirts.

I had felt sure the skirt was going to ride up at any moment, even though it fell to just above my knees, modest by the standards of high school. My blouse clung to me in a way that my comfy t-shirts never had. I longed for the bagginess of them. I barely recognized my reflection in the mirror as I donned my new outfit, but I didn't entirely hate the result.

"Remember not to fidget," mom had called as I shut the car door, hoping to drown out any further words of wisdom.

Against mom's advice, I kept reaching down to make sure the skirt had not slipped out of place. But my hands fell when I looked up to find the cutest boy I'd ever seen—staring at me. After a moment, he smirked slightly and gave me a wink making me go, I was sure, as red as mom's after an hour of jogging.

A beautiful girl with caramel-colored hair turned to see where the boy's wink had landed, and she met my eyes with such confidence and curiosity that I had no choice but to avert my eyes.

It was on my way to lunch that she found me. "Nice skirt," the girl said, falling into step easily beside me. "I've got the same one at home. I totally love it."

She was different somehow; it was in the way she spoke and moved. Everything deliberate, as if she were a competitor in a game.

"Why don't you sit with me today?" she suggested when I kept my silence. Upon entering the lunchroom, she steered me to a table in the center of the lunchroom. The center table was sure to catch the attention of everyone in the room. But before I could object, we arrived, encountering two girls already seated. They were beautiful like her, and I suddenly wished I had allowed Mom to show me how to apply makeup all those times she'd tried to pique my interest.

"Girls, this is Candace."

I felt uneasy, realizing I'd never given her my name. As if sensing a question was coming, the girl shrugged. "I asked some guy in my Math class who you were. I saw you grab Luke's attention this morning, and if he noticed you, others will too. So I've decided we need to be friends." She nodded with a confident smile, like the matter had been settled.

"I'm Drea by the way," she had said.

And that name had been all it had taken for me to follow her down a path there was no coming back from.

***

Looking at the clothes in my closet, the ones I used to love that had transformed me in more ways than one, I shook my head at the ridiculousness of it all. Had I just dressed in my normal clothing that first day of high school, would my life now be earth-shatteringly different? Would I still have had Shannon? Would I still have known who I was?

"Are you ready?" mom asked.

She stood just inside the doorway of my room with a tight smile. Today was going to be hard for me, but it would also test her.

I took a last, longing look at the clothes I had decided to leave behind. I hadn't worn them since my falling out with Drea, but it still sucked to abandon them.

"Ready as I'll ever be," I said and grabbed my suitcase from the bed. I cast a glance around at my room; I was going to miss it. My bed with my down comforter would feel strange to me when I got back, the way it did the first night after an extended vacation, but I was not going on vacation.

I expected mom to lead me downstairs, but instead she wrapped her arms around me. I didn't resist falling into the safety of her embrace. If there was one good thing that had come out of my friendship with Drea, it was that it brought me closer to my mother.

"Let's get moving," she said into my hair. I followed her out to the car, trying to drink in the home I was leaving for the next few months. These hallways and rooms were a part of me; I could list everything in them. I wondered if it would feel like a foreign land when I returned.

As we pulled out of the driveway, I felt like I was standing on a cliff and everyone was asking me to jump.

"I don't have to go. They can find someone else, and I can stay here," mom said again. The car ride had gone smoothly up until then, but I had known it would come up again.

"No, you can't," I said. "It's only a few months. I'll survive in the Stepford house somehow."

"Your father is excited to have you," she said tightly.

I tried to look as neutral as possible. I hadn't told mom about the conditions of my stay with dad. It wouldn't go well if I did. She had been surprised when I suggested about switching the game plan, maybe even looked a little hurt, but she hadn't objected.

The car ride to Dad's was less than ten minutes, but I wished for it to be a bit longer, not minding when we hit the red lights that normally drove me crazy. The trees were almost completely bare and the turned and dying leaves were clumped and scattered on the ground. Halloween was only a few days away. Most of the houses were decorated accordingly.

When we pulled into the driveway, I quickly checked how many cars were in the open garage. When I saw just one, I let out a breath I didn't know I'd been holding. The house looked exactly as I remembered it: too big for just three people.

The front door opened to reveal my father, who must have been waiting for me. I pictured him peering out the window just like he had at the old house when Austin had missed curfew.

Mom reached over and squeezed my hand, attempting to help ease whatever anxiety I felt. If she only knew that dad was actually the least of my worries.

"I'll walk you to the door," Mom said, and moved to release her seatbelt.

"No, mom. It's okay. You don't have to."

I hadn't spent a night in this house since dad had moved in, and now I had to spend a few months. I was giving dad an inch, but what if I wasn't able to stop him if he took a mile?

"I love you," I said.

I turned away from her slightly, hoping to hide my tears. They wouldn't make the next part any easier. Mom pulled me into the tightest embrace I'd ever known, and all I wanted was to never let go, but keeping her here was not an option. When I pulled back, I pretended not to notice mom's tears or my own.

I stepped out of the car and opened the back door to grab my bags. I didn't look back at her as I walked up the front walkway. I was too afraid I might run back to her.

Dad's arm twitched when I came into hugging range, but I kept my arms locked to my sides, not giving him any invitation to touch me, especially when the last person to touch me was Mom. Without looking at him, I turned and waved goodbye, and felt so incredibly alone as her car backed out of the driveway.

Turning expectantly to dad, I saw that he was just as uncomfortable as I. Watching him scramble for things to say momentarily threw me. He was always so confident and so sure, so unlike the person before me. He was the Vice President of a marketing company; Walt Ellis didn't falter.

"So how was the drive?" He crossed his arms and stood in his power stance. He had taught it to me years ago. Legs were spread wide. Back was abnormally straight. *It doesn't matter if you don't feel confident. All that matters is that you look it,* he had said.

"Considering it was only ten minutes, I guess it was fine." I looked around, pretending to be bored instead of scared. I felt a bit like an orphan dropped off with a distant relative. In movies like that, they usually formed a close bond and it all worked out, but my life never worked out like in the movies.

The front entryway, or "lobby" as May called it, still looked a bit like a museum. Vases, the kind not meant to really hold flowers, were perched on expensive tables, and the floors were abnormally shiny. How they kept everything so clean was a mystery to me. It was all just too…white.

"I could show you around," he offered.

"I already know the ins and outs of this house, or have you forgotten that?" It made me angrier than I thought it would to see him stand in this house like he'd been here first, when we both knew differently. I had been here for years before him, when another man had been the head of household.

He had the grace to look embarrassed. “How about I show you where you’re sleeping?”

“The pool house or the servants quarters?” I quipped, unable to dial back the sarcasm. Although now that I thought about it, the pool house was bigger than most people’s houses, and would probably be the ideal spot for me.

Dad barked an awkward laugh. He moved to grab my bags, but I picked them up before he could. He looked like he might take them from me, but just shook his head instead and moved toward the staircase.

As he led me upstairs, I laid my hand on the polished banister and remembered how I used to try to slide down it.

The pictures on the walls had changed. Dad was now in a few instead of Mr. Parker. There was no family portrait, though, which surprised me. This home used to have more family portraits lining the walls than any I knew. Perhaps Dad hadn’t been welcomed in that far yet.

We walked down the hallway and stopped at the room at the end of the hall. My new bedroom was the second guest bedroom. I remembered it vaguely, but couldn’t remember ever staying a night in it. I’d always stayed in Drea’s room with her. Months ago this all would have been a dream come true for us. It would have been the most epic of slumber parties.

The room itself was nothing extraordinary. The far wall was lined with windows. There wasn’t much of a view, and thick tree branches scraped against the glass, but a good amount of light got in.

Carrying my bag to the bed, I couldn’t help feeling twinges of jealousy. Everything in here was new: the off-white paint job, the bed, the dark wooden desk in the corner, and the armchair by the window. New. All of it. Just like Dad’s life. I was the one out of place.

The room had it’s own bathroom, which I was thankful for. Running into other occupants of the house while in a towel did not sound appealing.

Dad lingered in the doorway of my new room, as if he wasn’t sure if he was welcome inside. He would wait there forever if he expected an invitation.

"If you're hungry, we could grab a bite. I'm not sure when everyone else will be back. They went to the mall to buy whatever it is you girls buy," he joked.

But only moments after he said it, the front door opened and closed.

"Looks like they're home," I said. Cool sweat broke out on the back of my neck, and I prayed it wouldn't leave visible marks on my sweater.

As the footsteps grew closer, I couldn't help but feel like I was in *Jaws*. Every clack of a heel signaled the approaching sharks, and all I could do was let them start circling.

May came into view first. Tanned and golden, with the same color hair as her daughter, she was every bit the trophy wife. May smiled at me as if she were actually happy I was there. She wore form-fitting black slacks and a shiny blouse, so unlike what my mother wore.

"Candace, it's so good to see you again." Her smile broadened even further, but she didn't move to enter the room.

A flash of caramel hair appeared outside of the door, followed by its owner. I had known this was coming, but my throat still closed up at the sight of her. Her knee-length boots and too-short-for-autumn dress flattered her figure as she approached.

"Hey, Candace." Drea smirked. "So happy you made it."

While May's smile was genuine, Drea's clearly wasn't. Her coming into my room was, I was certain, a power move. This was Drea's house, and I was the unwanted guest. She opened my suitcase with a quick flip of her hand and examined my clothes.

Too quickly, I grabbed the framed photo of Austin and me from the top of the pile.

"Happy to be here," I said weakly, mentally calculating the days left until my mom came home. I clutched the framed photo to my chest as if it could bring me strength.

Dinner was awkward to say the least. It seemed everyone, except of course Drea, appeared to be tiptoeing on ice, unsure of what step would cause the crack to make us all fall through.

"So Candace, how is senior year going for you?" May asked, once all of the food had been laid out. She looked around the obnoxious candleholders in the center of the table to see me.

“It’s going,” I said and nibbled on my salad. I’m sure it was delicious, but it went down like sawdust. What was I suppose to say? My senior year had been an absolute nightmare, and her daughter had made it all possible? Somehow I knew May wasn’t looking for that kind of truth.

“That’s great. I know school can be stressful.” She looked to my father for what was probably his input, but he stayed silent. “Do you want some of the pasta? It’s really quite good. White sauce always seems to hit the spot more than red, but if you like red, I can make it for you next time.” She gave me a hopeful smile.

Before the affair, May had been like a second mother to me, and it made hating her incredibly hard, but it also made her betrayal so much worse.

“No, I’m actually not that hungry, but thanks.”

“You should have some pasta. I know you’ve been saying you need to diet, but really the weight you’ve gained is barely noticeable,” Drea said, smiling devilishly as May’s eyes swung my way.

“What’s this about a diet? You’re skin and bone,” Dad said with a frown, but continued to keep his eyes on his food.

“Walt, you know how girls are. Very conscious of their image at all that. Why when I was in high school …”

As much as I wanted to listen to May relive her glory years, I tuned her out the best I could. I only had eyes for Drea. I searched her for any sign of the person who had once been my friend. It was impossible to believe we had once been close enough to trust each other.

“Classes are going okay? Drea has been struggling in English this year, but we all agreed that if she applied herself, maybe read a bit more, she could bring up her grade.”

“Mom,” Drea almost growled in warning.

“Honey, I just think maybe if you asked for help, you could succeed.” May reached over to pat Drea’s arm. “Say, don’t you really enjoy English, Candace? Maybe you could help Drea!” She beamed like the idea was the best she had ever had.

“Mom, I highly doubt Candace has time to help me in English when she has been struggling in Chemistry all year.” She looked at me, daring me to deny it.

"Is this true?" Dad asked and put down his fork. I now had his full attention. Apparently, grades were more important than his pasta.

"I do better with some labs than others." More like I did better with some partners than others. I shot a look at Drea's smirk and had the strange, childish urge to stick out my tongue.

"If you still want to go to Dartmouth, you're going to have to work harder. Maybe ask for extra help," he suggested.

I snorted. He knew nothing of my struggles this year. I would have loved to have told him that half the reason why I was struggling was because I somehow kept getting partnered with Sean, who barely recognized we were in chem class, or Mindy, who had ruined two labs intentionally to sabotage me.

"Dartmouth?" Drea laughed. "Don't you have to be, like, super smart to get in there?"

"I get straight A's, Drea," I said, casting my eyes downward.

Throughout our friendship, I'd been very careful to never discuss my grades with my friends. It had been easy to hide them, as Drea never actually seemed to care about her own.

"No, you don't," she insisted.

"Yes, I do. You know I'm in all AP classes, and I've gotten A's in all of them so far. With the exception of Chemistry, I guess."

Drea's face was one of contemplation, but gave nothing away. "Jesus. You're one of the Top Ten."

"I wish you had told me you had been struggling. I would have tried to help you," Dad continued, oblivious.

The tension around the table got the better of me. "Why would I ever trust you to help me?"

Drea put down her fork with glinting eyes as if this was what she had been waiting for.

Dad opened his mouth to respond, but May touched his arm, and he simply lowered his head. The power of her touch baffled me. We sat in silence for a few more minutes before it became unbearable.

"I've got to work tonight," I said. I moved to grab my plate, but May waved me off.

"Don't worry about it. I'll take care of it." She kept her smile, even though some of the light behind her eyes vanished.

As I walked out of the dining room, I almost turned back to say something to Dad, but decided against it. I wasn't sorry for anything I had said, so I stiffened my back and my resolve. He'd never apologized for breaking up our family, so why should I apologize for the truth?

CHAPTER 5

"So how was the first day in the dragon's lair?" Joe asked when I clocked in.

"Meh. It was fine. There was some strategic bomb-throwing over dinner, but all in all it could have been worse, and probably will be at some point. I'm counting my blessings today." I put my jacket and purse in the break room and came out to the concession counter.

"That's the spirit." He took a quick look over his shoulder toward Robby's office. "At least your afternoon was eventful. I've been stuck here with Robby, who by the way I am pretty sure is going through a breakup because he has been extra dickish, and he only gets that way when his new girl leaves him."

"How do you figure that?" I grabbed cleaner for the tops of the counters and began spraying them down. If Robby did happen to come out, it would look better if I looked busy.

"When you've been working with Robby for as long as I have, you come to understand that none of his girls work out. They come and they go just as quickly. I think it's because he has mommy issues, but I've never been brave enough to ask."

"And you're telling me all of this because…?"

"Because…he assigned you to train that new kid, and I'm afraid he may watch you like a hawk, so he'll have someone to take his frustration out on." He began wiping down the counters with me, which was a blatant move to soften me up.

"New kid?" I asked, straightening up.

"Yeah, that guy from the other night. Mark?"

Mark. Shannon's friend Mark.

"Why am I training him and not you or Rachel?" I'd never trained anyone before, and I didn't particularly want to train Mark. His friendship with Shannon made me feel completely uneasy.

"Rachel is off tonight. Something about babysitting her brother…and I may or may not have volunteered you to train him after I saw you talking to the group he was with the other night," he said innocently. He placed his hands in the air when I rounded on him.

"You did what?" I said. "*Why*? Why would you do that?" I grabbed the spray I had been using on the counter and advanced on him.

He brought his hands to his face to shield his eyes. "If you're going to spray it, don't get my face. It's too pretty to go out like this."

Weighing my options, I huffed and put the bottle down.

He peeked out from behind his fingers and slowly lowered his hands. "I just thought maybe it wouldn't hurt for you to interact with someone your own age. You know, make a friend or something. I hate to say it, but you're kinda on a shortage."

"Gee, when you put it that way," I muttered, leaning back against the counter.

"That's not what I meant. You know I think you're great, and maybe other people will too if you give them a chance to get to know you and see you aren't a walking clone of Drea, you know, anymore. Also, it wouldn't hurt to maybe have some male attention." He edged closer slowly, like he was still afraid I would spray him.

"I don't need male attention. I have you and you give me plenty of attention." Okay, true, I hadn't had any male attention since Luke. But I was fine with that. Luke hadn't exactly been kind when he left me, and I just didn't feel ready.

"Girl, it's not the same and you know it. You're wonderful, but you're not my type. If you were, I'd be on you so fast." He pushed his hip into mine gently, making me laugh. Joe made it no secret that if he'd been into girls, he would date me, but according to him, he hadn't dated girls since the ninth grade. It was a true loss for women everywhere. His blond hair, gray eyes, and muscular frame frequently caused quite a flurry when single ladies hopped in his line.

"Speaking of types, how was your date last night?" I asked, hoping to direct the conversation away from *my* love life.

"It came and went. He was cute and all, but I love me a man with substance, you know? I mean he doesn't have to read Aristotle or anything, but he definitely needs to know who Adele is."

"Yes. I, too, believe Adele is in the realm of Aristotle."

"Don't we all. And don't think I didn't notice your little change of subject."

"What do you want me to do?" I sighed.

"Just give him a chance to get to know you. The real you, not the one you were, and if he extends the olive branch, please take it. You need friends, Candace." His look of concern made my heart melt a bit.

I hadn't even thought to put myself out there. I wanted to be invisible. Every bridge I'd built had been burned when Drea had taken me down.

"You don't get it. Kids at school hate me. Mark shot daggers my way the other day; he's friends with Shannon."

He wrapped his arm around my shoulder and gave me a gentle squeeze. "I'm not exactly sure what the big deal about Shannon is, but you can't let it destroy you. You hurt some people, but you'll never know if people can forgive you if you don't put yourself out there. How many interactions have you had with this kid?"

I ran through my history with Mark, which didn't take long. There wasn't much there. "We've had a couple classes together over the years, but I don't think we've actually had a conversation."

"Then he's perfect," he said matter-of-factly. "If you haven't really talked, then he has no firsthand experience to judge you."

I was sure he had probably heard enough about me to make up his mind, but there was no changing Joe's mind. "Fine. I'll train him, and I'll try to make a friend. God, that sounds so stupid."

"Nah, listening to Robby all day makes you sound like a genius to me."

I shoved him playfully as Mark came in through the front door. Just the sight of him made me want to go back on what I had just agreed upon with Joe, but if I didn't try now, I didn't know if I ever would.

To say that Mark looked apprehensive when Robby told him I would be his trainer was putting it mildly. The distaste when he found we were to be glued to the hip all night was all over his face. Oh yeah, he definitely knew all about me.

"I thought she just started working here. Shouldn't someone with experience be training me?" he asked without looking at me.

How did he know when I started working here?

"Candace has been here long enough. She knows what she's doing. Listen to her and you'll be fine," Robby said with a tone of finality. Turning to me, he said, "Any problems, I'm in my office."

Funny, I thought. He'd said the same thing when Rachel had trained me…

I stood there for a beat, a little unsure of what my next move would be.

Joe gave a slight cough behind me to get me moving.

"Okay, so the first thing you want to do is punch in," I said, gesturing toward one of the computers.

"Robby already had me do that," Mark said curtly. His look of unhappiness deepened, and I swore I would never let Joe talk me into anything like this ever again.

"Okay, then. The next step is to assess the floor. See if the people working concession need help—that's mostly on weekend evenings because we tend to get super busy. We're on through close tonight, so I'll take you through all the cleaning stuff when it comes time. Right now, we can hop on the counter and start taking orders, so I can show you how to ring everything up."

"Sounds good," he said, keeping his dark eyes focused on anything but me.

As we moved up to the counter, Joe took a place not too far down and gave me the thumbs up before taking someone's order. Good to know he thought I was impressive, because Mark surely did not.

As far as training went, Mark was a quick study. He picked up the computer system faster than I had, and he was a lot more comfortable talking to customers. I noticed things about him when I watched him search the computer or the counter for something, and saw the way his brow crinkled when he wasn't sure or couldn't find something. It was almost cute or something. Not that I was interested in someone who clearly hated me.

He seemed to hate asking for help, or maybe he just hated asking *me* for help because he always let out a breath before looking my way. I took it as a little victory that he was at least talking to me. This making friends thing was totally not as easy as Joe had made it out to be.

When it was our break time, I showed him the break room and wasn't surprised when his nose crinkled.

"You get used to the smell. You know that short kid, Vic? He takes his breaks in here and eats chilidogs every time. It should dissipate in a bit." I smiled at him and tried to breathe through my mouth to avoid the smell.

"I get to leave for my break if I want, right?" He looked around briefly at the chairs and sofa, but made no move to sit on any of them.

"Yep. You have half an hour to do whatever you want. I sometimes go down to the bookstore on the corner. They have really comfy chairs, or the corner market makes pretty good milkshakes." I tried to make my voice sound neutral, like I didn't care either way if he stayed with me.

He nodded and moved to grab his jacket. He had it buttoned and was out the door before I had even finished.

"I guess I'll see you after break," I called with all the false cheer I could muster.

This whole being nice thing left a lot of room for hurt feelings. Joe would have been so disappointed to see me in that moment. Alone and pathetic. Alone was how I usually was, but it felt worse today.

I looked at the chair I usually sat in to do my homework. I could sit here with the smell of chilidogs, or I could head to the bookstore. It was open until eleven tonight. I loved the way it smelled. It probably sounded odd to some, but it smelled like experience and adventure, so unlike my life.

I grabbed my jacket and made the short walk to the bookstore. The wet leaves on the ground made the walk to the store a slow one. Autumn was beautiful in Brinkerville, but it was still a pain to avoid sliding on wet leaves.

"Candace, you haven't been in to see me for ages," Vincent complained, as he spotted me from behind the counter. He was a tall man with thinning gray hair, dark eyes and a contagious smile.

I felt my mouth pull up just by looking at him.

"I came in three days ago. I'd hardly call that ages." I hung my jacket on the coatrack, thinking how long the three days had actually seemed. Every day passed like dog years for me now.

"Well, it gets lonely in here, and not many people come in who actually want to read. Just the ones who need a book to pretend to read for whatever useless class they're taking," he said and sorted a stack of books on the counter.

"How do you know they pretend to read them?" I asked.

"Because they return them a couple weeks after they buy them. They let the teacher see they have them, use them for papers or whatever, and then they return them."

"Maybe you should change your return policy then," I suggested and went over to the New Additions shelves.

"Maybe, maybe," he said, rubbing his chin. "Tea this evening? My son just made it. Oh, my son! I've been wanting you to meet him, remember? He's the only one who reads as much as you do. Though you wouldn't believe it because he's never actually *here.* Doesn't want the cool kids to know his dad owns a bookstore I guess."

"I doubt that's the reason, but I'm actually on a time crunch. I'm on break from work, and I was hoping to grab a book or two for the week," I said. He spoke of his son often, but I really wasn't in the mood to be set up, which I was pretty sure was Vincent's angle.

"That's fine. He just started working at the theater. You might know him already," he said, and indicated my work uniform. "Just hold on, okay?" With that, Vincent sped from the room.

I tried to stop him, but he was already gone when I called after him. I had the sudden urge to flee before he came back. The theater only had one new employee, and I was positive he wasn't going to want me here. I thought back to my many conversations with Vincent. Had he ever mentioned his son's name? He must have, but to my embarrassment I couldn't remember.

As much as I wanted to run, another part of me wanted to stand my ground. I'd been run out of the cafeteria at school, out of my relationship and my friendships, but I would not be run out of here.

I tried to distract myself with the things that had always provided an escape for me: books. Unsure of what to pick up, I perused the young adult section. I had just finished *Far From the Maddening Crowd* and *Water for Elephants*, and I wanted to change it up a bit. I'd fallen in love with young-adult lit after reading my first Sarah Dessen book. When I brought up YA books in my AP lit classes, some of my teachers gave me superior looks, like it wasn't a worthy genre, but I knew better.

I picked up one new one from an author I wasn't familiar with as Vincent came back into the room with none other than Mark trailing behind him, and while Vincent beamed, it was hard to miss how Mark glared my way.

"My son Mark!" Vincent gestured to him proudly.

"Hey, Mark. Long time no see," I said, offering him a small wave.

Mark kept his eyes on his father, like if he didn't look at me, I would disappear. Vincent's brows crinkled.

"We go to school together," Mark sighed. After a beat, he added suspiciously, "Didn't she tell you what school she went to?"

"I actually didn't, and he never asked," I said before Vincent could respond. It had never come up. The bookstore was located just on the edge of Brinkerville. It was easy to let Vincent believe I was from another town and went to another school.

"It's a small world," said Vincent.

"Well Brinkerville isn't exactly know for being a big town," I said, trying and failing to ease the awkwardness. "My break is almost over. I think I'm going to go with this one." I placed the book on the counter.

"Ah yes. I just got this one in. You'll give me a review when you're finished?" Vincent said as he rang up my purchase.

"Absolutely." I noticed Mark roll his eyes at the title of my book, but hey, sometimes romances novels just hit the spot. I took the book from him, my head swimming with the knowledge that I wouldn't be visiting the store anytime soon, if at all ever again. Mark would surely tell his father all about me.

"Mark, your break must almost be over. Why don't you walk Candace back?"

"Oh, no. It's not far, and he still has a couple minutes," I protested and quickly grabbed my jacket and flung it on.

"You shouldn't walk alone at night. It doesn't matter how far it is. Mark?" Vincent looked at his son in a "you better get moving, now" way and smiled as he and I exited the shop.

A cold gust of wind caught me off guard as I opened the door to the outside. The nights were getting far colder, and my body still wasn't ready for the chilly weather.

Mark's jaw worked back and forth as he walked next to me. His eyes, so like his father's that I felt stupid for not recognizing the resemblance, were trained ahead like he was looking into the future and hated what he saw. I wondered if he saw me.

I pulled my jacket tighter, not quite sure if the chill was from the weather or the boy next to me. I was almost resigned to remain in total silence, but I found myself explaining, "I didn't know Vincent was your dad. He's been talking about you for months, wanting me to meet you. It's funny," I said, and my breath came out like smoke.

He stopped abruptly and turned to me. He had the kind of eyes you would find the devil wearing at a crossroads.

"What exactly is it that you think you're doing?" he asked quietly.

"Walking back to the theater?"

"No, I mean with trying to make conversation all night? It's like you're trying to be friends with me or something."

"I was just trying to be nice," I said and wrapped my arms around my chest.

"You're not nice," he said slowly. "You've *never* been nice. You used to spend your days taking down other people. Hell, I watched you laugh when you made Violet Banning cry for talking to someone's boyfriend."

I winced slightly at the memory of her scrambling to collect the photos. Mark had watched me do that? Just when I'd thought nothing could make that memory worse.

"You've never even talked to me. You don't know me enough to assume anything about my character," I retorted, although my heart wasn't in it.

"I know you more than I'd like to. You're a self-absorbed, mean girl who puts everyone else down, so you can come out on top. But your friends dropped you, your boyfriend dropped you, and now you're alone and looking for someone, anyone to ease your sad existence."

"If I were looking for someone, it wouldn't be you," I said coldly.

I expected him to show a bit of hurt at my comment. Instead, he just smiled a sad smile. "There's the girl who stalked the hallways."

My face flushed. “I didn’t stalk anything, and I’m not that person. I’m not…self-absorbed.”

“Yeah? How many classes have we had together?”

“What does that have to do with anything?”

“How many classes have we had together?” he repeated and put his hands in the pockets of his coat, looking like he had all the time in the world.

Gritting my teeth, I thought back. We’d had heath class, and chem class, and maybe one English class together. I couldn’t picture him in any of my other classes, but I had a sinking feeling that he knew my answer would be wrong.

“Three,” I said, knowing I was wrong the moment the number left my lips.

He laughed quietly and shook his head. “We have been in the same core classes for the past two years. Tell me again that you’re not self-absorbed.”

Instead of arguing, I decided enough was enough. I’d promised Joe to try and I had, even though I’d failed. “Listen I… I didn’t mean to offend you by talking to you. I just thought since we’re going to work together, we could converse or whatever, but that’s my mistake,” I said and started to walk away.

“How could you think we could do anything when you’re the reason Shannon did what she did,” he called.

His words rooted me to the spot. I stood immobile as what he said registered. For so long, people had whispered about it. That I was the reason Shannon had done what she did. Rachel had alluded to it the other night, but it had been a long time since I’d heard it in full, and time had done nothing to take away the sting.

Turning to him, I bit out, “Fuck you, Mark.” Mark’s eyebrows jumped slightly. I surprised him. Good. “You didn’t know me before. You don’t know me now. You don’t get to judge me.” I tucked my hands into the pockets of my coat and made the journey back to work. I added an extra hustle to my step to escape Mark and the cold he brought with him.

CHAPTER 6

I never thought I would be thankful to pull into my father's new driveway, but I felt relief at the sight of it. The rest of my shift had gone by in a tense wave. I had told Mark what he needed to know, but stopped there, and he seemed to make a conscious effort to put at least five feet between us at all times. Joe had tried to talk to me before the end of his shift, but thankfully I'd had been too busy.

When I got out of the car, I saw the light on in the study. The relief I had felt when I pulled up was gone. I knew without going inside that my father was waiting up for me, like he had done with Austin years ago.

I opened and closed the front door gently, hoping to sneak past Dad without him noticing my arrival home. Luck, however, was not on my side. Dad called out to me when I had only taken a few steps across the front hall.

My heart sank. Hadn't we talked enough over dinner? Hadn't that been painful enough?

When I entered the study, he was occupying an armchair right by the window. He'd watched the car pull in; I never had a chance of getting by him. On the small coffee table in front of him were two mugs and a teapot.

My breath failed me for a moment as took in the sight, and I bit my lip to keep it from trembling. Perhaps if I clamped down hard enough, the emotions I felt would stay behind my teeth.

The scene was a familiar one, but it felt like a lifetime since I'd last seen it. It was so similar to what I remembered, but so drastically, tragically different at the same time.

"You're up late," I said when I was sure my voice wouldn't betray my emotions.

"Couldn't sleep knowing that you weren't home yet." He put the stack of papers he was holding on the coffee table. "I've got tea if you're not too tired. Chamomile. Your favorite." He pointed to the teapot in front of him. His smile was a hopeful one, and it made the wrinkles around his eyes more prominent.

"I switched to coffee," I said tiredly.

His smile flickered. I saw the question forming in his mind: when had I started liking what I used to refer to as "mud juice"?

Dartmouth. Think of Dartmouth. "I guess I could have a cup," I said and sank into the unoccupied armchair.

I blew on my tea before taking a sip. The taste brought back the memories of when we used to sit together, drinking tea and reading books. I'd been jealous of his relationship with Austin then, so I'd taken it as a chance to bond with him. Austin and dad had had finance and sports, but we'd shared tea and books, and I'd always believed our bond to be stronger.

"Do you always work so late?" he asked.

"Most weekends I do," I said.

"It must be tiring. Working so much." He looked at me with something like worry.

"It keeps me busy." It kept me from feeling too lonely, too, but I wasn't about to tell him that.

It occurred to me that he was probably just as uncomfortable as I was. We had gone to dinner plenty of times before this, but I'd never had something I wanted so desperately on the line.

"How's Luke?"

His very name brought with it a fire that I had to swallow back. "We broke up." I didn't know if it was the mention of Luke's name or that dad had no idea how bad things had gotten for me when he'd blown my life apart, but I felt my anger surge.

"Well, that's too bad." He tried his best to put on a sorrowful expression, but I guessed he was actually relieved. Dad had never been Luke's biggest fan, not that he ever said anything like that to me. I could tell though. Whenever Luke had blown me off, dad was the first one to swoop in to cheer me up. "Now you have a bit more time for school. Dartmouth means dedication."

"I'm dedicated. My application is going out in a couple weeks." I'd also be sending them to some safety schools. Dartmouth was the dream, but dreams weren't cheap, sometimes they weren't even affordable.

"They'll be lucky to have you," he said confidently. "Let me know when the acceptance letter comes in, so we can plan a celebratory dinner."

I snorted. "That presumptive. The letter might be a rejection."

"I doubt it. You've always done everything you set your mind to."

"We'll see," I said and tried not to let his kind words penetrate too deeply. He had a way with words, but I reminded myself that nothing he said could be trusted. His compliments would create chinks in my armor if I wasn't careful.

"I've got the tuition check ready to go."

The mention of the money made my stomach roll. It reminded me that I had made a deal with the devil.

"If I behave right?" I said harshly. I placed my teacup down on the table and got up to leave.

"I'm trying here, Candace. I really am. I just want to be a part of your life again. You may not believe me, but I'm happy you're here with me." He looked down at his own cup, making his expression hard to read.

I paused in the doorway of the study and turned toward him. "You left me. I can't forget that."

"I left your mother, not you," he sighed. He sounded exasperated, and he probably was. He'd said the same line so many times.

"You left me the same day you left her," I said softly. "You broke my life into more pieces then you could ever imagine. I'm just now putting those pieces back together, and I'm not ready to fix the pieces involving you yet."

He nodded slowly. "Will you ever be ready?"

Guilt rose within me. He had caused so much pain, but it still felt like a knife in the gut to know I'd caused him any. "I don't know," I whispered.

"I hope you will be." He turned away from me and became very fascinated with whatever he saw outside the window. I wondered briefly if he was crying, but if he was, I didn't want to see.

I fought tears all the way to my bedroom. The moment I shut the door behind me, a sob broke from my chest. I sank into my bed and buried my face in a pillow to muffle the sounds.

Sitting with him had been a mistake. I'd been able to handle my anger, my rage, but my feelings of missing him surprised me. They were buried so deep that I'd forgotten them. Part of me felt wrong for missing him. How could I miss the man who had sparked the fire that burned my life to ashes?

I took a breath to calm myself down. Dealing with all of this after the day I'd had was too much. I went to the bathroom and splashed warm water on my face and brushed my teeth. When I finished, I felt calm enough to try to sleep.

I slipped into my bed and pulled the covers over my head. I felt tired enough that sleep should have come quickly, but it evaded me while thoughts of Dad, college tuition, and Mark's harsh words rode a merry-go-round in my head.

I had finally begun to drift off when there was a scratching noise on my window. I'd heard the branches of the tree outside making similar sounds earlier, so I rolled over to chase the sleep that ran faster from me with every passing moment.

It was when I heard the window creak open that I shot up in bed. My heart began to pound as I squinted into the darkness. It was dark, but my eyes had adjusted enough to see a figure crawling inside. I opened my mouth to scream, but no sound came out. My body was stuck to the bed, my legs locked, my whole being consumed with fear.

There weren't break-ins in this community, ever, and now one was happening on my first night in my new bedroom.

Snatching a hardcover book on the nightstand, I hurled it at the figure now standing inside the window. The moment the book left my fingertips, I bolted from the bed toward the door, and I tried again to scream, but again it was lodged in my throat.

"Fuck. My nose," a voice groaned in the dark.

I'd just whipped open my door when that voice stopped me. That voice. I knew that voice. That voice used to be the one I loved to hear the most, but what the hell was he doing here?

I shut the door lightly and flicked the light switch.

"Fuck," Luke repeated. He clutched his nose in his hand and glared at me. Dark red blood seeped through his fingertips.

"What the hell are you doing?" I demanded, finally able to find words. My heart still pounded in my chest.

"None of your business." He tried to sneer, but failed spectacularly as he still had his nose in his hand. A wounded Goliath. The part of me that wanted vengeance for every bit of shit I put up with, while he'd stood idly by, felt a sick sense of victory.

I went to the bathroom and grabbed a dark-colored washcloth. I wanted to avoid having to explain to May why there was blood on her towels.

"You just climbed through my window. I think that warrants an explanation." I tossed the washcloth at him and took care to leave space between us. He caught it with one hand while the other still clasped his nose. He carefully put the cloth to his nose and tried to mop up the blood.

"I'm not here for you. You just have the tree outside your window," he said, as if his final destination should have been obvious.

It took me a few seconds to understand his words. He'd come to see Drea.

"I suppose it's good you haven't lost your ability to climb trees and crawl into your girlfriend's windows." After all, it hadn't been that long since the last time he'd crawled through mine.

Luke looked down and avoided my eyes. He staggered a bit, and it was then that I noticed the smell of booze wafting off of him.

I heard fast-approaching footsteps and almost told Luke to hide. My parents had never caught Luke in my bedroom, and I forgot for a moment that he wasn't my boyfriend anymore. Now it didn't matter. What did I care if Luke got caught in here? I would only have to explain that after we broke up, he'd started hooking up with Drea, which would come as a surprise to Dad since he had no idea Luke and I had even broken up before tonight.

It was not Dad, however, who burst through my door; it was Drea.

"What are you trying to do, wake up the whole house?" she demanded. Even in pajama shorts that read *Pink* across the butt, she looked gorgeous.

Looking at Luke, I saw that I wasn't the only one who noticed how well Drea wore her clothes. I reminded myself that Drea had carefully picked out that outfit, as I looked down at my baggy sweatpants and t-shirt with mild mortification.

"What happened to your face?" Drea asked as she moved to Luke. In an anything but tender way, she inspected the source of the blood.

"She threw a book at me," Luke accused and winced when Drea shoved the washcloth back into place.

Drea rounded on me with blazing eyes, and I was pretty sure it was the first time she noticed my presence.

"Oh yeah. Like throwing something at a creep sneaking into my bedroom at night, IN THE DARK, is my fault."

Instead of responding to me, Drea turned back to Luke and said in a mildly annoyed tone, "I told you to wait for me to come and open the window for you."

"I got bored. You were taking forever." Luke pulled the cloth away from his face and lightly touched his nose. Most likely wondering if he was still beautiful.

"Whatever. Just do what I say next time. I'm shocked you didn't wake everyone up." She extended her hand, and he took it willingly.

Watching Drea lead Luke out of the room reminded me of a mother leading away a sulking child. The thought caught me off guard and I tried, not too successfully, to cover my laugh with a cough.

Drea allowed Luke to go out of the room ahead of her and paused in the doorway. "Laughing at what a joke your life has become?" she said, addressing me for the first time.

"Something like that," I said coolly.

"I'm glad you finally find it as funny as the rest of us do." She smirked. "Luke will be visiting again in a few hours, so try to refrain from throwing your lamp or something at him."

A few hours? After he and Drea had done God-knows-what to each other, he was going to parade through my room? "Um. No, he won't. I'm going to bed."

"That's too bad. This is *my* house, so whatever I say goes." She brushed her hair over her shoulder as she twisted around to walk down the hallway.

My blood boiled. I was stuck in this house, in this room, but Drea didn't get to dictate what happened in it, especially if it concerned Luke.

I walked to the door and called after her, not bothering to keep my voice down. "As long as I am forced to stay here, this is *my* room, and sorry, but you don't get to parade my leftovers through my window because you want to be groped by my ex-boyfriend."

Drea stopped walking and her back visibly tensed. Perhaps she was stunned by my will to fight back. As she turned, she said, "Do you really want to do this with me, Candace?" Drea approached the doorway, looking every bit like a panther ready to pounce.

On my list of wants, fighting with Drea was at the far bottom, but I'd taken enough bullshit for one day. I straightened my back and my resolve. "I'm not arguing with you. I'm telling you that Luke crawled through my window enough times when he was my boyfriend, so I want to be spared the sloppy-seconds show."

Drea's eyes widened, and she opened her mouth to spew something vile. Something that would most likely tear away any confidence I had left, so instead of listening to it, I slammed the door in her face. It was a coward's move, but it was the only one I had in terms of survival.

I quickly locked the door and listened as Drea tried desperately to turn the handle. The door moved as she kicked at the other side.

"This isn't over," she said on the other side of the door.

In a moment, I heard her move away, and I let out a steadying breath. Drea could probably sneak Luke out the front door if she timed everything perfectly—Dad had probably gone to bed. But he sometimes had trouble sleeping. I'd often heard him rummaging around the house for things in the early hours of the morning.

There was a good chance Luke and Drea would be caught. I felt guilty for wanting it as much as I did. I wasn't jealous. I was long past that. The two of them carried on like I had never even been a part of their lives. It had taken me time to even *want* to move on without them, and they'd replaced me so quickly. That part still stung when I thought about it.

I shut the open window and locked it. I made a mental note to make sure it was locked every night. I didn't care if Drea snuck Luke in every night, as long as it wasn't through my window.

CHAPTER 7

I wasn't quite sure how the Monday morning routines worked at the Stepford mansion, so I'd set my alarm for earlier than I was used to. Bleary eyed, I fumbled my way through a quick shower and barely looked at the sweater I picked out to wear with jeans. I gave myself a quick glance in the mirror. The outfit was forgettable. Exactly the look I wanted.

I'd cried the first time I'd broken the morning routine Drea had taught me. I was boring and plain without it. My blond hair didn't shine as much and my eyes weren't highlighted to look like smooth chocolate. My looks had drawn attention before. I used to love that. Now, it was my nightmare.

I had planned to sneak downstairs and rummage around for a granola bar, but dad was waiting for me in the kitchen when I got there.

"Hey, I'm making pancakes. Your favorite!" Dad said.

I hadn't seen my dad in a kitchen before. With his tall frame and broad shoulders, he looked almost too big for it. A burning smelled filled the air.

"Actually, I'm in a rush this morning. I'm just going to grab a granola bar or something," I said as I took in the blackened food in the pan.

"Oh okay. No problem. I'll just eat this." He looked at the pan dubiously.

"I'm surprised you're here. Don't you usually head into the office early on the weekdays?" I said, while I looked through the cabinets.

"When I can. May likes me to be home in the mornings, so we can eat breakfast together."

"Well, it must be nice to find someone to change for." I wanted nothing more than to get out of there before May came in for a family breakfast.

"Candace…" He sighed.

I held up my hands to prevent us from going down the same road as the other night. "Yeah, I know. I'm heading to school."

"Wait, why don't you and Drea ride together? You could wait for her," he suggested.

It was hard to remember that he was only trying to help. He had no idea that he was asking me to ride in hell's hearse with Drea.

"As fun as that sounds, I'm going to walk. It's only about a thirty-minute walk from here."

"That's if you speed walk," he laughed. "There's no point in walking; just wait for Drea."

"Dad, you've been out of the picture for a bit now, so it'll come as a surprise to you that Drea and I aren't as close as we used to be. I don't want to ride with her, so just let it go. Okay?" I gave him only what I needed to so I could get out of there. I picked up my coat and backpack and readied myself for my walk.

"Wait." He slid a set of keys across the counter. "Here, take my car again. I'll take the Camaro. The BMW can be yours while you stay here. And Candace, Drea told us about you pulling away from her. What happened between your mother and me wasn't her fault, so ease up on her okay? She's going through a lot."

He placed the pan in the sink and walked out of the kitchen, leaving me to wonder how the hell I had become the bad guy.

I made it a habit to get to school a bit early on Mondays. Sometimes people messed with my locker on Fridays, so I just liked to check out any damage before I had an audience. Once I assessed my locker, which appeared to be untouched, I decided to sit in the chem classroom and go over my notes.

I had a quiz this morning and didn't feel confident in the concepts. The quiz was on the lab we'd just done, and that one had been a particular disaster thanks to Mindy's helping hand. I never actually failed the quizzes; mostly I got low B's, but there was no way Darmouth would take grades like that.

Students slowly started filtering in, but I kept my head buried in my notes. When the stool beside me shifted, I didn't need to look up to know Mindy was there. Her floral perfume had alerted me to her presence when she was still in the hallway.

Mark and Shannon walked in together a moment later. I tried to keep my eyes down, but they shifted to him as he passed. He kept his eyes straight ahead, but for some reason, Shannon's swung my way. She hadn't looked at me, really looked at me like I was alive, in years.

As I stared back, Mark's words form the night before played in my mind. *You're the reason*. I had the sudden urge to ask her, to know finally if I was, but I couldn't. I didn't think I'd be able to live with myself if it had all really been my fault. Ignorance was my ally, here.

"Okay, I'm going to hand out the quiz, and then you need to start on the next chapter," Mr. Mason announced. "Answer the questions on this sheet. I'll try to get the quizzes back to you before the bell."

I whipped around and tried to cram just a bit more. It was a futile effort. I would have struggled on the quiz even if Mindy weren't next to me. Every time I blocked my quiz with my elbow, Mindy kicked me under the table or knocked my arm after she checked to make sure that Mr. Mason was enthralled in the papers before him. When I handed the sheet in, I knew the score wasn't what I needed to bring my grade up.

Toward the end of the class, Mr. Mason called me up to his desk. A few people laughed quietly as one kid made the *DUN DUN DUN* sound. He thought he was clever. I, however, thought he was a fool.

"Candace, normally I don't call students up to discuss grades above failing, but I've heard from your guidance counselor that you have a certain college in mind. Perhaps this class is too hard for you? Perhaps a tutor would help?" Mr. Mason stared at me over the top of his wireframe glasses.

Ms. Weatherbee's contact with Mr. Mason didn't surprise me. She made it a habit all year of touching base with my teachers. I wasn't really sure why, but I guessed word had spread about my home life.

I didn't realize I was nodding until I head Mr. Mason call out, "Mark, can you come up here for a minute."

Both Mark and Shannon looked up from their work at the same time. Mark looked suspicious as he approached the front. If being up here wasn't humiliating enough, having Mark as a witness to my shortcomings was the cherry on the sundae. Behind Mark, Shannon kept staring.

"Mark, Candace is in need of a tutor, and I think you would be great for it. What do you think?"

Mark shot me a dark glance and opened his mouth to respond, but Mr. Mason said, "Good! It's settled then." He ushered us off with a wave of his hand and bent his head back to the papers in front of him.

I made a note in my mind to beg Ms. Weatherbee to stop trying to help me.

As I walked back to my seat I was careful to keep my gaze down. I tried to concentrate on the work in front of me, but between Mindy mocking me for needing a tutor and the feeling of being watched by my classmates, focus was impossible.

I snuck a peek behind me and found Mark and Shannon whispering. I couldn't help but feel that it was about me. They were probably strategizing a way for Mark to get out of helping me; maybe they were talking about everything I had done to Shannon. Just the memories tore at my heart. It wasn't hard to point to the moment when our friendship had disintegrated.

Shannon had been out of school the entire first week of ninth grade. It hadn't been unusual; she was always ill. Seven days had been enough to build a bridge between Drea and me, and enough to break the supports of the one between Shannon and me.

When Shannon, wearing a *Pokémon* shirt and boy jeans, had approached our lunch table, I'd nearly choked on my sandwich.

"Candace, why don't you shove down and make some room for your friend," Drea had said silkily.

I hesitated, but then relented. Shannon sat right next to me, but for the first time since we'd met, she didn't seem to fit there.

"Hi! I've heard so much about you from Candace. She says she really loves hanging out with you. I'm Shannon." Her sentences ran together, the way they did when she was excited. "You're in my English class, right?"

"Yeah," Mindy said coldly, "aren't you the one who shared the love poem?"

"It was actually a Haiku. I wanted to do a whole poem, but for some reason a Haiku made more sense. What did you do for your summer reading assignment?"

"A book report. You know, like everyone else in the class." Beside her, Allison let out a giggle, but a look from Drea quickly muffled it.

"What an interesting shirt you have on there. From the Salvation Army?" Drea questioned and Mindy and Allison both giggled.

Looking almost thoroughly confused, Shannon looked at her shirt as if to make sure she had indeed put on the right one that morning. "No, my mom got this for me from Old Navy. Candace has the same one. We got them to match." She smiled and elbowed me.

"My dad got the shirt for my brother, not me. I only wore it around the neighborhood to make her feel better," I burst out. "Honestly, I wouldn't be caught dead wearing something like that."

I watched Drea's mouth quirk up and Shannon's head dip, eyes filling. The crowd at the surrounding tables had grown quite. Their heads all tilted to listen in.

"Why would you say that, Candace?" Shannon whispered like I had taken her voice, not just her dignity.

"I'm tired of looking ridiculous to spare your feelings." My tone was stone cold, leaving no room for rebuttal or argument.

It had taken everything I had to keep my face impassive as Shannon shot from her seat and ran out of the lunchroom. Drea, Mindy, and Allison's laughter, and the surrounding crowd had followed her tears the whole way.

"You did the right thing," Drea had said and touched my arm, in one small showing of sympathy.

Looking at Shannon as she sat with Mark now, I wished the memories away, or at the very least, for my hand in her torment to have ended with the cruel words in the cafeteria.

When the bell sounded, Mark was beside my lab table. "Did you ask him for me to tutor you?" he whispered and looked over to make sure Mr. Mason was occupied.

"Of course not. I was just as surprised as you," I said. I gathered my books and looked him straight in the eyes. "You made your opinion of me quite clear last night."

I meant to walk away with what was left of my dignity, but I failed to notice Mindy, just outside the door and out of view of Mr. Mason, shoot out her foot. My notes spilled from my notebook as I flung it to free my hands, so I could catch my fall. Pain shot up my wrist as my hands made contact with the cold, unforgiving floor.

"Oops. You should really be more careful." Mindy cackled and leaned casually against a set of lockers.

When I looked up, I saw Allison, Mindy and Drew crowded tightly together, wearing predatory smiles. Drew's brown hair shot out at odd angles from under his ball cap, making him look just a bit deranged. He kicked my notebook out of reach when I made a grab for it and let out a humorless laugh.

"Stop it, Drew," I said and made fruitless grabs for the paper he kicked and crunched. The hallway floor was littered with scraps.

"What do you expect, Candace? Luke's my best friend. You think I'd let you pull shit and get away with it?" He sneered and put his face in mine. I had the urge to pull back away from his rancid breath, but backing down or showing fear would give him a victory. Intimidation was his favorite tactic.

"I didn't pull anything, asshole. I didn't *do* anything!"

"Keep telling yourself that. But we all know, slut." With a final stomp on my torn and crumpled papers, he, Mindy, and Allison left me to clean the mess.

Other students in the hallway gave me space like my condition was contagious, like they knew my position could be theirs tomorrow.

I grasped desperately for the pieces of paper around me. Tears stung my eyes as I tried to swallow the lump in my throat. I would not cry. Not here. Not where people could see.

When I turned to look for my actual notebook, I saw a hand extended toward me, holding it. Mark crouched next to me, looking like he wasn't sure whether or not he wanted to duck back into Mr. Mason's room for help.

"What did you do to them? Why do they hate you so much?" he asked as I took the notebook from him. He reached for a few other papers, but I waved him off.

I laughed bitterly. "That's the best part. I didn't do anything to them."

The way he looked at me while I was down on my knees, defeated, drove me crazy.

"Why do you care, Mark? According to you, I'm pretty much the worst person ever," I spat.

He recoiled from me and stood. He looked for a moment like he was going to say something, but instead he shook his head

"Mark! Are you ready?" Shannon called. She stood only a couple feet behind him looking impassively at me like the scene didn't surprise or shake her, and why should it? She should be reveling in my pain. God knows I would have if our situations were reversed.

"Yeah," he said and turned to me. "I'm sorry, I can't help you."

He started to walk away when I called, "Can't help me in chem or life?"

He stopped suddenly and turned to contemplate my question. Behind him, Shannon tapped her foot impatiently. Mark stared at me for so long that I thought he wasn't going to answer. It wasn't until I stuffed my notebook into my backpack and got up to make my way to second period, that he did. "Both."

Chapter 8

What goes around comes around. That was the phrase I couldn't help but repeat to myself, over and over, when I stared at the link waiting for me in my email.

Drea hadn't always been like this, not all the time. I'd loved her, once. For the moments when she'd cared, *really* cared. It had been Drea who comforted me all the times Luke had broken my heart. She had stroked my hair and promised he'd be back. It had been those moments, the soft ones that had made me believe Drea was a good person underneath it all.

She had been softer with me, but inside our school, she had shown no mercy. After Shannon had entered Drea's radar that day in the cafeteria, Drea had taken extra steps to torture her. She'd spread rumors about her, tacked ugly notes to her locker, and made sure everyone knew that Shannon Bowen was a loser.

Once, after learning that Shannon was afraid of snakes, she'd had Drew open the top of Willy the python's cage during their shared zoology class. I hadn't seen Shannon that day, but I'd heard she'd spent the day in Ms. Weatherbee's office crying. Perhaps torturing Shannon had been Drea's way of testing my loyalty.

Everything with Shannon came to a crescendo the week of finals in ninth grade. Instead of studying for her history exam, Drea had expected that Shannon would let her copy; even after Drea had made it clear she was nothing more than dirt to her. Drea's rude awakening came the day of the exam.

"I can't believe she didn't let me copy," Drea had seethed. "Now I'm going to have to explain why I failed the history exam to my mother. I'm going to make her life hell. I swear when I'm done she's going to have nightmares bad enough to make her sleep in her parents' bed every night."

"Well, you can't do that because her parents sleep in separate beds." I didn't know what made me reveal something Shannon had told me in confidence. When we had been children, Shannon rarely spoke about her parents. It had been like they were off limits somehow. She'd never said it, but I knew the topic of her parents was her Achilles heel.

"Her parents don't even sleep in the same room? That's fantastic. What, do they hate each other or something? Is her dad gay? No, don't tell me, it doesn't matter," Drea squealed.

That night I got a message in my email account from an unknown sender. Believing it to be junk, I almost deleted it, but the subject made me hesitate. It read: *About That Bowen Girl.*

When I clicked the link provided, it sent me to a new site. In the middle of the page was a picture of Shannon in a beanie and Batmant-shirt. The picture wasn't flattering. The red hair that stuck out of the beanie was wild and frizzy. Her makeup-free face was covered in angry-looking acne. Above her picture were the words, *Who is Shannon Bowen?* And just below there was a button to click.

I clicked on the page, and it led to a new cite. One with a blurb about Shannon, along with a comments section. "Shannon is an ninth grade girl, whose parents do not sleep in the same room. Why? Well, the theories are…" The theories ranged from her parents hating each other to her father actually being gay—her mother being his cover so no one would know he had a preference for younger children. By the time I'd scrolled down to the comments, there were already over fifty.

The whole families fucked up.

Daughter of a pedophile…no wonder she's so out there.

Our classmates had not been kind that night, but what sent a jab through me was that Shannon had been one of the recipients of the email.

I'd gone to bed that night feeling like Judas. It had taken fear and popularity for me to trade in someone who had once been my greatest friend. The next day at school, I'd kept a lookout for Shannon. Why? I hadn't known. I couldn't take anything back, and it hadn't been like I would have traded all that I had gained to apologize to her. In the end, it had been useless to look for Shannon that day. Word had spread by lunch that she'd been hospitalized. She'd swallowed a bottle of pills late in the night.

For reasons unbeknownst to either of us, there were no consequences for Drea or me. It was like no one dared to say what

Drea had done to Shannon. What I had helped her do. But my classmates had looked at me differently after that, like I had shoved the pills down her throat.

Now as I sat at my desk with my email pulled up, I realized I was getting what I deserved. I'd helped Drea humiliate Shannon, and now Drea was using the same tactics on me. Emails with links like the one in front of me came every now and then. Usually, they sent me to a fake social media account or a message board. Whatever the destination, it was always ugly.

The first had been the picture of me with Mindy's brother. The one Luke had shoved at me, and it had earned me the title of slut. Sometimes there weren't pictures at all. Sometimes it was just comments. The comments were anonymous, but I knew Drea, Mindy, and Allison were behind the first few.

The slut at work.

Did you see the bump on her lip the other day? Herpes for sure.

Derek said she was the worst lay ever.

I wasn't even sure I knew a Derek.

The rest of the links kind of blended together. They all had the same message: I was a slut and trash, and anyone who hung out with me was the same.

The link I looked at now was to a message board labeled "Truth from Candace's Fuck Buddies," and although the title was new, the comments weren't. There was talk of getting t-shirts made, so all the guys I'd supposedly slept with could be easily identified. Maybe it shouldn't have bothered me as much as it did to read them, but Luke was the only guy I'd ever been with.

Feeling low, I turned off my computer and got into bed. Deep down I knew it was right, in a way, what was happening to me. I was paying penance, and I would continue to pay it, even if absolution was nowhere in sight.

Chapter 9

"Is this one any good?" I asked and held up a book from Joe's bookshelf. It didn't compare to the vast array Vincent's store had, but I was working with what I had.

The bookshelf looked out of place compared to the rest of the apartment. Books were crammed in at odd angles and spilled out slightly. He stacked others on top. Looking at this, people would never believe how orderly Joe kept everything else. His desk was immaculate and dishes never sat longer than a few minutes in the sink.

"Stephen King is always good. That one will take a while to get through, but the ending is worth it. You know, now that I think about it Drea kind of reminds me of Pennywise, draining life from others and all that, perhaps it might be too scary for you," he said, wiggling his eyebrows.

"Maybe," I laughed and stuffed the book in my bag.

"My books are your books. Get anything new from the Vincent's Bookstore lately? Anything you would want to lend me that is?" He looked at me expectantly.

I averted my eyes. I'd avoided telling him about my self-imposed exile because he would make it a big deal, which is wasn't. "I haven't been in for about a week."

"You've got to be kidding," he said. "You're letting Mark run you off?" He sat up in his desk chair, ready for his cross-examination.

When I'd first told Joe about my evening with Mark, he'd been furious, and I'd been grateful to him for his loyalty. The truth was I didn't blame Mark for the way he felt, not really. Even though I'd expressed that to Joe, he'd treated Mark coolly since then anyway.

"I'm not *letting* him do anything," I argued. But I did miss the bookstore. The smell of the books. The comfy chairs. Vincent, who now probably thought I was the worst.

"Yes, you are. Poor Vincent. It's not like pretty, smart girls walk into his bookstore everyday."

"Don't be a perv. Vincent is sweet, not a creep." I punched his arm.

He raised his arm as if he were actually hurt. "I know. I know. I was just playing. No need for violence. But I do think you're being undeniably stupid for not going back into the store. Who cares if Mark is his son? Mark's not the nicest kid."

"He's not the nicest person to me because he's seen me at my worst. Yeah, what he said sucked, but whatever. I'll get over it." I tried to sound nonchalant, but knew I hadn't quite achieved it in my tone.

"Mhmm. Sure. You can pretend all you want, but I've seen the heart in you. It always sucks when people say shit. Even if some of it is true. I'm sorry I pushed you to talk to him in the first place. I thought it would be good for you, but that backfired, huh?" He looked at me apologetically.

"Meh. It's not your fault. I was a troll and now I'm paying the price. I just don't want to go in to see Vincent and have him hate me." I plopped down on his bed and leaned back into the comfy pillows.

"Why would he?"

"Because Mark probably told him all about me. I loved that Vincent believed I was a good person. Sure, he thought that because he knew nothing about me, but it was nice to have a clean slate with someone, you know?"

He nodded sympathetically. "You are a good person. Who knows, maybe he won't care about what his son says." He came to lie down next to me. Our arms touched, and I had a feeling of peace. With everything in my life going wonky, Joe was a pleasant constant.

"Maybe," I agreed, but didn't really believe it.

"Well, well. I knew you were just pretending to be gay." Dave chuckled as his muscular figure enveloped the doorway.

"Yes, this was my plan all along. Come out in high school pretend to be gay for five years and lure unsuspecting teenage girls to my bed. You got me." Joe leaned up on his elbows to look at his roommate.

"Thought so. Candace is way too pretty to be ignored," he said, smiling down at me.

I blushed. Dave was always saying stuff like that when I was around. I wasn't special. I knew that. I'd seen him with other girls he'd bring over. He was a player, so I took it in stride.

"How was the gym?" Joe asked, ignoring my red cheeks.

"Not bad. Didn't get as much time in as I wanted, but that's all right. Want to grab food or are you working tonight?" He flexed his muscles slightly, and I had the sneaking suspicion it was for my benefit.

"Miraculously, I have been given a Friday night off."

"You want to join, Candace?" Dave asked.

"I wish, but I'm working." I pouted and sat up to check the time on my phone.

"Our loss. I love eating dinner with beautiful women," he schmoozed.

"She's in high school," Joe chided. He got off the bed to shove Dave out and shut the door. "And you, take that smile off your face. He's a player and you know it."

"I know. I know. He's just so sexy all the time. How does he do that?"

"Maybe he's born with it. Maybe it's whatever the ending to that commercial is." He began to rifle through his drawers for a new shirt.

"Yeah, well either way he's a good-looking man. I suppose I should get moving," I said and grabbed my jacket.

"Don't let anyone at work get you down. You know, in case anyone who has recently given you a hard time is working tonight." He gave me an almost guilty look.

"You checked the schedule, didn't you?" I stopped buttoning my jacket.

"Of course. I was shocked I had a Friday night off and wanted to know who Robby had put in my place." He shrugged into his new shirt and checked his reflection in the mirror.

"Well, who is it?"

"Mark," he said with an apologetic smile

Of course it was. With my luck, it could only have been him.

***

I cursed Robby for giving Joe the night off as I rang up another buttered popcorn. Didn't people know extra butter clogs arteries? I wasn't jealous of Joe. It wasn't like I had anywhere to be, and I needed the money, but I would choose comfy yoga pants instead of being sandwiched at the concession counter between Rachel and Mark any day of the week.

So far they'd managed to avoid actually acknowledging me. If Rachel had something to say, she dramatically leaned around me to say it to Mark. Mark wasn't so overt, but he didn't do anything to actually make me feel wanted either.

The last rush was almost over. The ten o'clock showings were the last the theater had tonight, which meant we'd be out just a touch after midnight. A few kids from school had come through my line, but most went to Mark's. He wasn't popular by Drea's standards, but he seemed to be liked by the kids who came into the theater. He made socializing look effortless in the way I had never felt it to be.

A new Matt Damon movie had just released, so we were extra busy. It surprised me that Luke hadn't come in. When we'd been dating, he would take me to see action movies. I'd gone without argument every time, even though I didn't care for them. Looking back, I'd been afraid even then that if I didn't do what he wanted, then he'd find another who would.

It wasn't until the lobby was almost completely empty that they all came in.

Mindy laughed at something Drew said. Allison looked, as usual, like she'd missed the joke. And right behind them, Drea bounced along next to Luke, their hands laced together, looking every bit the happy, golden couple. I wondered if that was what I'd looked like when it had been me who had held his hand. Had I looked golden? I'd certainly felt that way.

Drea's bounciness increased when she saw me, and her eyes sparkled as she directed the group into my line. It was like the lion pack approaching the antelope. I kept my eyes trained on Luke, hoping to see just a flicker of the boy I'd loved. Maybe he would take pity on me.

"We need a large Coke and a medium popcorn," she ordered and clicked her perfectly manicured nails on the counter—black, to match her soul. She wore designer black jeans and a pink blouse. Everything on her was wrinkle-free and perfect. She fit next to Luke in a way I didn't anymore.

I didn't look at her as I poured the Coke and scooped the popcorn, and I tried not to grimace at the amount of butter on my work shirt. When I placed the Coke on the counter, Drea snatched a straw and smashed it into the top of the cup. A moment after her lips touched around the straw, she pushed the soda away from her. "I asked for diet Coke, not regular," she said loud enough for everyone working concession to hear.

I closed my eyes and willed myself to find patience. When Drea shoved the cup even further toward me, like I was her personal servant, the last of my patience vanished. Maybe it was the way one of Drea's hands was still interlocked with Luke's. Maybe it was the way she flaunted him in front of me, like it was all just a game.

"No, you didn't. You ordered regular. I'm sorry you're having trouble remembering an event from one minute ago," I said, trying and failing slightly to keep my voice even.

Out of the corner of my eye I saw Rachel and Mark, both free of any customers and too curious to not look, turn toward me.

Drea's bounciness stopped then and her expression transformed to one of deep indignation. She picked up the soda slowly, like she were weighing it in her hands, and for a moment I thought she was actually going to take it and walk away. "You may drink regular soda, but some of us actually care about how we look. From the size of your love handles we can all see you don't."

Then she extended her arm, grinned at me, and let the soda slip from her fingers. The cup fell at such an angle that when it landed on the counter, the lid flew from the top, and soda exploded from it, covering the counter and my work uniform. There were speckles of sticky-sweet soda on my face. I felt their cold rivulets trickling down to my neck, but the coldness did nothing to ease the lava burning within me.

"I am so sorry," Drea squealed and made a show of handing me a single white napkin. Everyone behind Drea laughed, except Luke, whose face was unreadable except for his eyes. His face and eyes hardened when he saw me looking.

"Is there a problem here? What's this mess?" Robby looked at the counter with deep annoyance.

"That girl basically threw her soda at Candace," Rachel said boldly, not backing down as Drea glowered at her.

Her quick defense of me sent a jolt of surprise through my body.

"That's not true at all! Candace gave me the wrong soda, and I was just handing it back to her when it slipped," Drea argued, followed by a chorus of protestation from Mindy Allison and Drew. Luke, however, still kept his silence.

"I suggest you all go to your showing, and you all clean up the mess," Robby ordered before going back into his office and closing the door. He was officially the worst boss ever.

"Your girlfriend stood up for you," Drea purred. "Isn't that nice! Although, I can't say I'm surprised you've decided to come out, Candace. After all, Luke said you were like a cold fish anytime he tried to put the moves on you."

Her smile widened when as redness invaded my face. She had said it to get to me. I knew she had. Luke, the boy I had loved, would never have said anything about our intimate moments, not when he knew what they meant to me.

"Drea! Let's go, *now*," Luke barked. He didn't bother looking over his shoulder to see if she would follow him. Every girl would have followed him. Even covered in soda and humiliation, I would have followed him.

Drea looked annoyed at his tone, but she felt confident enough to give me the finger before walking off with her minions in her wake.

"Lovely," Rachel muttered. She grabbed a cloth and began wiping down the counter. "You know, before you started working here there were a lot fewer messes to clean up."

"You think I asked for this? You think I love to be their favorite target?" I grabbed another cloth and began helping her, putting more force into it than necessary.

"You think I asked to be labeled a dyke for my entire high school experience? We all have shit, idiot. Deal with it and move on."

"Oh yeah, it sounds like you've moved on," I shot back.

With that, Rachel slammed the cloth on the counter and headed for the break room.

I don't know what possessed me, but I called, "I'm sorry I did that to you."

Rachel's body went ridged. Her arm was outstretched, hand clasped around the doorknob.

I'd wanted to apologize to her before, but I didn't—for the fear that she would laugh in my face. Seeing her frozen like that made me unsure about continuing, but I felt compelled.

"I was afraid of losing Luke. I hated you for having his attention, really I hated anyone else who had it. It's not an excuse at all. I was a terrible, terrible person. I was insecure and… you don't have to forgive me, but I'm sorry." I clamped my mouth shut to keep from rambling further. I waited in silence, at Rachel's mercy. She could tell me to pound sand, and I wouldn't have blamed her.

Rachel turned and crossed her arms. "You and your friends made my life hell."

"I know," I said and looked down at the washcloth I was still holding.

She gave me the up and down before uncrossing her arms. "I still don't really like you, but you're hard to hate when you're covered in soda." She turned to walk away and threw over her shoulder, "Thanks for the apology, Candace."

The door to the break room closed behind her. I didn't know if anything would change between us or if she'd stop looking at me like I was a fly in her coffee, but I felt lighter. That was something at least.

I moved to grab the spray cleaner to finish cleaning off the counter, but Mark beat me to it. He bent down next to me and sprayed the cleaner and began scrubbing the counter with me.

"Thanks," I said focusing on the counter.

He nodded. "Your old friends are assholes."

"Yeah, they can't help it. They were born that way." Out of the corner of my eye, I saw his mouth quirk up. I still didn't know what to make of him, but the way his mouth moved sent a pleasant twist to my stomach. It wasn't much, but I'd take it.

CHAPTER 10

Lucifer must have been in charge of making high school students' schedules. It was really and truly the only explanation for a first period chemistry class.

"Find your partners," Mr. Mason called, sending a chorus of groans through the class.

My groan was probably loudest of all. I was dead in the water the moment Mindy sat down next to me. I got out my notebook and pretended to be heavily invested in my lab packet, while trying not to envision Dartmouth slipping further and further away.

"Need a partner?" a voice deeper than Mindy's asked from beside me. I turned and saw Mark in black-framed glasses, jeans, and black t-shirt, looking relaxed as if the offer was one he made everyday. Without waiting for a response, he sat down in the chair next to me and pulled his notebook from his backpack.

"Really?" I asked. "What about Shannon?" I looked back and saw Shannon partnered with Mindy. While Shannon's face was impassive, Mindy's was one of deep annoyance.

"Don't worry. If Mindy tries to mess anything up, Shannon will annihilate her. She takes chemistry very seriously," Mark said with a shrug.

"Okay, eyes up here," Mr. Mason directed. "We're going to start a lab on how electricity changes pH. It'll take up a couple of days to get through everything. Be careful to not short out the batteries. They'll get hot, so be careful. Make sure all your safety gear is in place before you start anything."

The class began to move, gathering lab gear and materials. When we returned to the table, Mark organized everything. He was in his element, and he looked sure and comfortable. He looked good, attractive even, when he was confident like this. "So do you want to record everything as we go?" he asked.

"You trust me with that?" I knew I was more than capable to complete the task, but I wasn't sure if Mark actually trusted any part of his grade to me.

"I doubt you're actually bad at chemistry. You didn't seem to struggle in our other science classes." He put on his safety goggles.

"You paid attention to me in other classes?" For some reason, the knowledge that he cared enough to notice me gave me a slight feeling of weightlessness—quickly followed by shame.

What was it he had said, that night we'd walked back to work from the bookstore? *We have been in the same core classes for the past two years. Tell me again that you're not self-absorbed.*

He hated me. What he was doing now was out of pity.

"That's not the point," he said quickly. "I think you can pull your own weight here. Am I wrong?"

I shook my head. "Okay, where do we start?" I pulled on my goggles. Even though they made everyone look ridiculous, I felt more ready to do a lab than I had all year.

The class passed quickly. Mark and I worked together well, and before long Mr. Mason was calling for us to clean our stations. "I'll copy everything I took down," I told him and couldn't help but smile. I felt confident about my work, and that hadn't happened all year.

"Sounds good," he said. "How are you doing with the concepts here?"

"Okay, actually. It's easier to record things properly when you have a good partner."

"Yeah, I guess so," he said. He looked down at his own notebook with his pen hovered over the lined page. "Do you still need a tutor?" There was hesitation in his voice.

I turned to him. "Are you serious? You said it wasn't going to happen."

"Maybe I changed my mind."

"Why are you doing this?" It seemed like too fast of a turn around to be genuine. My gut told me to trust Mark, but my gut had been wrong too many times to be relied upon.

"Can't you just let someone help you?" When I just stared at him, he huffed, "Fine. My dad might have encouraged me to help you. Apparently, he has a very high opinion of you." He looked at me like he was trying to see what his father saw.

"I thought you would have told him all about me by now, and he would hate me."

"I did. When I got home from work my first night, he wanted to know why I was cold to you in the store, and I told him everything I knew about you, which you know, isn't exactly great. You know what he told me? He told me it didn't matter. He said you went into that store two to three times a week, and you were one of the nicest people who walked in there." He shook his head as if his father's words still confused him.

"Is that all?" I pressed.

He let out a breath. "He also said that I should help you because even though I don't care for you, it's the right thing to do."

"So you're helping me because your dad is making you?" I accused. "Listen, I don't need your pity or charity, okay? I'll be fine on my own."

I tried to stand, but he reached for me and laid a hand on my arm. His touch was gentle, feather light on my skin and maybe that was what made me pause. He removed his it quickly, like he hadn't meant to touch me. "I'm helping you because you need it. I don't pity you. Well, maybe I did at first, but I don't now. Watching you with Drea yesterday, and your apology to Rachel…I didn't think you had a side like that."

I sat fully back and assessed him. If I let him help me, I would have a better chance at Dartmouth. But there was still the feeling that it would be wrong somehow. I looked back at Shannon and found her looking at us. She looked away quickly when our eyes met.

"What about Shannon?" I whispered. "You don't think this would make her uncomfortable?"

He looked unsure at the mention of Shannon, but said, "She actually thinks I should help you."

"What?"

"Believe me, it shocked me too," he said.

It struck me that this all might be some scheme for Shannon to get retribution, but I didn't think so. Even though Shannon and I hadn't spoken in years, it just didn't seem like something she would do. Drea. Definitely. Shannon. I doubted it.

"I really do need help," I said finally.

"Good." He smiled. "Just so you know, it was hard to argue with those clear goggle marks on your face."

I frowned. "What exactly do you think your face looks like?"

Later in the day, Mark found me in the library during lunch period. I was surprised at first to see him and worried, for a moment, he'd changed his mind. He put my mind at ease when he took out his notebook.

When he was going over notes from the previous week, he looked up and found me looking at him.

"What?" he asked.

"I'm just wondering why you're giving up your lunch period to help me."

"I'm not," he said and took a sandwich from his backpack. "I brought it with me. Besides, you need to refresh on what you didn't catch last week before the quiz tomorrow."

"Okay." I listened to him while he went through what I hadn't caught when Mindy had been my partner. It was easy to notice how steady Mark's voice was when he relayed information. He didn't judge me when I asked him to go back over something or make me feel stupid. By the end of our first session, I felt better than I had all year in terms of chemistry.

"Same time Thursday?" he asked as he packed up his bag.

"That would be amazing," I said. "Thank you for doing this."

"No problem," he said, and after a beat added, "How are you after this weekend?"

"You mean with Drea and them? I'm fine." When he quirked an eyebrow at me, I laughed. "As fine as fine can be I guess."

"They seem to have a special liking for you." He meant it as a joke, I knew he did by the way he rolled his eyes, but what came out of me wasn't a giggle or chuckle, it was a strangled cry. It surprised us both, and it was all I could do to bury my mortified face into my hands as tears fell into them.

"Oh shit. I'm sorry. I didn't mean to…please don't cry. I'm an idiot." The steadiness of his voice was gone, replaced by mild panic. It was almost enough to make me laugh. Dad, Luke and even Austin had struggled with solutions when I'd cried it front of them. Too much emotion seemed to be boys' kryptonite.

"You have nothing to be sorry for," I mumbled through my fingers. I took a steadying breath and wiped a few tears from my cheeks, lowering my hands only when I knew no more would escape. "I'm the one who's sorry. I don't normally burst into tears. I swear."

"It's all good," he said with a slight wave, like the last few minutes could be erased with a flick of his hand. "We all break sometimes. Honestly, I'm shocked you don't cry more. When they carved *bitch* into your locker at the beginning of the year, I thought for sure you would, but you just looked at it and went to class. Like it didn't matter to you at all." He didn't quite smile at me, but he looked at me with something like admiration.

"I wanted to cry that day. I went home and did," I admitted. I didn't know why I was confessing my weakness, but in that moment it felt okay, right even. "I try not to let them see it here; it just makes it worse, so I save it. I bury it, and only let it come out when I'm somewhere safe. Although, I don't know where that place is anymore since I had to move in with Drea. It's like living in the hornet's nest."

"You live with Drea?" His eyebrows scrunched together, like he was missing a piece of the puzzle that was my life.

"I just recently moved in. My dad lives with her mom, and my mom went away for work, so I'm there until just before Christmas."

"Your dad and Drea's mom are together?" When I nodded, he grimaced. "Family dinners must be something to look forward to."

"They are something. We skirt around each other, which makes it all so awkward. I can barely look at my dad since everything happened," I stopped just short of telling him everything. The urged to welled up within me. I hadn't told anyone, not even Luke. I didn't know Mark well. I didn't even know if he'd even stopped hating me, but something inside me pushed the words from my mouth, as if a part of me already trusted him. "My dad cheated on my mom," I whispered. The moment I released the words, it was like a floodgate opened and everything came pouring out: my father's affair, Drea's hatred, and Luke's belief that I had betrayed him. When I finished, I sucked in a breath and waited for his judgment.

Mark sat with his hands on the table. He didn't speak for several moments. "That's fucked up," he said.

I couldn't help but laugh. It was blunt and honest and entirely what I needed. "Yeah, it kind of is." After a moment, I sobered. "Sometimes I think I deserve it. Drea's goal was to make everyone hate me, but a lot of people did already. I made them feel that way all on my own."

"No one deserves what those assholes deal out." When I smiled wryly, he said, "What? You disagree?"

"No, but it seemed like you were kind of okay with it on your first night of work."

He ducked his head a bit. "I felt guilty the whole night after I said those things to you. You were being so nice, but I wanted to hate you for the things you've done. I was resolved to hate you. But that's not me. I'm not a person who likes to hurt others."

"It doesn't matter," I say. "Some of it was true."

"I told Shannon about it," he confessed. "We've been friends for years, and it was the first time she's ever been mad at me."

"Mad at *you*?"

"Yeah. She said I had no business saying any of that to you, and that what happened back then was complicated," he said, still looking like he didn't understand Shannon at all.

"Did she—" I started, but my voice failed. My fear that I'd been the reason Shannon had tried to kill herself still haunted me. It crossed my mind every time I saw her. I didn't want to know, not really, but part of me needed to. "Did she ever say why she did it?"

I didn't need to say what I meant by *it*. Mark understood. "No. I asked her once after it happened, but she just said she didn't want to talk about it. She never said it was because of you, if that's what you want to know."

I let out a breath I didn't know I had been holding. The axe lifted from my neck, but it still hovered there. Just because she hadn't said it didn't mean I was free of blame.

"I miss her," I said, without meaning to. Of all the things I'd told him today, it felt like the most intimate.

I waited for him to laugh or ridicule me. What rite did I have to miss the girl I'd helped destroy?

"I think she misses you to," he admitted rather reluctantly, like he wasn't sure if the admission was a betrayal. "She never says so, but she watches you sometimes when she thinks the rest of us aren't looking."

“Do you think she’d forgive me?” I kept my voice small, so he wouldn’t know my hopes were big.

“If anyone could forgive you, it’d be her.”

Chapter 11

I spent the following days thinking of how right Mark had been when he had called me self-absorbed that night outside the bookstore. He was in my English, chem and math classes this year. How could I have missed him? It wasn't like he was quiet or shy in class. He readily raised his hand and confidently gave answers, and he asked the questions everyone else needed answers to, but were too afraid of looking incompetent to actually ask.

Ever since he had accused me of not noticing anyone but myself, I'd taken stock of those around me. I was embarrassed to find I had most of the same people in all of my classes. With the notable exception of Mindy, who had only made it into my chem class because she had cheated off of Alex for three years.

I found myself wishing I had more classes with Shannon. We took the same level classes, but our schedules didn't align. Chemistry was the only time we were in the same room together, and I was more than aware of how Shannon watched Mark and me when we worked together. It wasn't hard to miss the frown on her face when Mark laughed at something I said. He and I were growing closer, almost close enough to call him a friend, and it seemed Shannon didn't love that, even though she'd wanted Mark to tutor me.

While chemistry and my progress in the friend department were going well, my home life was still a struggle. I'd managed to survive just over a couple weeks without any massive blowouts with dad, but I wasn't sure how many more family dinners I could sit through. May was an excellent cook, so the food was always something to look forward to, and for the most part Drea refrained from throwing me under busses. We usually didn't speak to each other directly, which was the preferred route, but it was still excruciatingly uncomfortable to sit there with the three of them.

It was May's suggestion to switch dinnertime on Fridays, and while I would have preferred to miss it, it was kind of nice to know she actually wanted me there and didn't just feel obligated. While May's suggestion was helpful, Dad had resorted to complaining about my work schedule.

"Have some fun!" he'd said when I'd gotten home from working a double. "I love your work ethic, but you don't even need to work. I'd be happy to give you an allowance so you could focus on school and maybe hang out with your friends."

"I like working," I'd said. "My guidance counselor told me it's important that I look well-rounded, and she thought a part-time job would show commitment to being an important member of society and such." It had been a lame lie, but it kept him off my back.

Tonight's Friday dinner seemed to stretch on longer than normal. Drea was heading to her father's right after, which usually put her in an extra bright mood, but she seemed distracted and disengaged. She was probably wondering if she'd packed enough shoes for two nights.

May and Dad were also abnormally quiet. They usually bombarded us with questions, but they barely asked us how the food was.

Their silence put me on edge. Something was off. I pushed my food around on my plate, until it was close enough to the time when I could leave for work. As I stood to excuse my from the table, May's head snapped up as if she'd just remembered we were all there.

"Oh Candace, you can't go yet. I made peanut butter cup pie. It's delicious—you have to have a piece. Sit down. It won't take more than a few minutes." May quickly disappeared into the kitchen.

I sat back down, bewildered by May's sudden exit. I looked to dad for an explanation, but he carefully avoided my stare.

Drea's eyes narrowed when May came galloping into the room. She had just set the pie down when Drea asked, "Who died?"

May and dad looked startled. I had the urge to laugh at the cartoonish way their eyes widened, but stifled it when I realized Drea wasn't joking.

"Why on earth would you ask something like that?" May said as she sat down. Her face a practiced mask of calm.

"Because the only time you make peanut butter cup pie is when someone dies."

"That is not true!" May laughed tensely and cut into the pie. She held the first slice out to me. I didn't take it.

"Actually, it is." Drea raised her hand to tick points off her finger. "You made it when Nana died, when we had to flush Nemo down the toilet, when auntie Mary—"

"Okay, okay. I get it," May said and held her hand up. She put the spatula and plate she was holding down.

My chest constricted when May didn't deny someone had died, but there was no way Dad would let something like that be shared over dinner. Perhaps they were separating and Dad had decided to come back home.

I held my breath as May took one to compose herself. They were breaking up. That was the only thing that could have them both so shaken.

"We have some news," she began and faltered when she looked at Drea. She looked to Dad for help, but his eyes were steadily examining the flickering candle in the center of the table. "We're going to be adding a member to this family," May said, so quietly I was sure I'd heard her wrong.

"What did you say?" I asked, voice shaking. I took my hands on off the table to clench them in my lap.

"We are going to have a baby. I'm pregnant." May might have been shaky on the lift off, but when she uttered the word "pregnant," she couldn't hide the smile that swept her face.

The world began to tilt. The word *pregnant* rang in my ear. A baby. Dad was going to have a baby with someone else. I was going to be a sister *again*, and all I could think about was Austin. Was that what this was? Did Dad think that he could replace Austin, and his life would be whole again?

I wasn't sure what May thought the reaction of the room would be, but I was positive that it wasn't Drea dropping her fork with a loud *CLANK* and looking like Luke revealed he was actually gay.

"You can't be pregnant!" Drea screamed, the pitch of her voice making May shrink back. "You're too old."

Dad slowly clasped May's hand in what I assumed was solidarity. His silence at dinner was now fully explained, but he still didn't even look at me. How could he sit there and say nothing, while I felt my already broken world shatter even more? There really was no hope he was ever going to come back to us. My life was never going back to how it had been.

"I'm only thirty-nine, honey. I was sure this would never happen. Your father and I had you when we were young, and we tried after we had you to have another baby, but it just never happened for us." May's eyes shone with tears.

"So you decided now was a great time to try again? Now when I'll be gone in a couple of months, you can just start all over with a new family!" Drea's breath was coming out fast, and I swore she was fighting back tears. It was the most human I'd ever seen her. She hadn't even cried when we'd caught our parents in the act. It opened up something in me that I never wanted to feel again—sympathy, for the girl who had ruined my life.

"That is not what happened. I didn't mean to get pregnant. It just happened," May's voice grew loud, not quite matching Drea's.

"It just *happened*?" Drea hissed. "Is that really the line you're going with? Do you understand how stupid you sound, Mom? Pregnancies don't just happen. I'm sorry that you weren't thinking enough to wrap it up before letting someone who isn't dad—"

"Drea, that's enough. You're out of line." May's small, free fist came down on the table, causing the whole thing to shake.

Unfazed by her mother's loss of composure, she continued. "Ha! I'm out of line? That's rich coming from the woman who cheated on her husband and is now pregnant. God, just when I thought my opinion of you couldn't get any lower." Drea threw her chair back and stood. "I'm going to Dad's. You know, where I'm a valued member of the family." She stormed out of the dining room and didn't look back.

The air in the dining room was thick. I should have probable gotten up too. The clock on the wall told me I was going to be late for work, but I couldn't move yet. I sat there waiting for Dad to look at me, to say something, anything.

"Candace, I'm so sorry if this causes you any pain," May hiccupped as tears rolled freely down her cheeks.

Sorry wouldn't cover the pain the two people before me have caused. In my junior year, we'd read *The Great Gatsby*, and as I looked May and Dad, I realized I understood now what careless people looked like.

Anger still coursed through me. I wanted to unleash it, but instead found myself asking, "How far along are you?"

At the sound of my voice, Dad's head popped up. I felt him looking at me. Finally.

May looked hesitant. "I'm actually about three months in. I'm not showing yet, thank goodness."

Three months? No, that would mean... I turned to Dad. "You knew about this before I moved in," I accused.

"We didn't want to say anything because we wanted to make sure nothing happened to the baby in the first couple months. May's putting her body through a lot to be pregnant now." His voice was plaintive, but the words Drea had uttered about starting a whole new family resonated with me. He was trying to replace the son he'd lost. He was trying to replace me.

"Does mom know?" I asked. At the mention of mom, Dad had the decency to look ashamed.

"I called her this morning. I asked her to let me tell you. I thought it would be better that way."

"Well, at least she knew before me *this* time," I said. Dad's face drained of the little color left in it. I stood and looked at May. "Congratulations, May."

"Candace, wait," Dad called, but I didn't look back. I couldn't. If I stayed, I knew I would do or say something that would lose me any chance at Dartmouth.

As much as I blamed May for my parents' divorce, I couldn't yell at her. It was hard to describe the way I felt about her on a normal day, but it was even harder now. The look on her face when she'd made her announcement had been one of almost pure joy.

As I went upstairs to change into my work clothes, I heard Drea slamming drawers in her room. We weren't on speaking terms, but did that mean we couldn't somehow help each other through this? Maybe this was what would bring us back together, or at least end the war.

I decided to bite the bullet and raised my hand to knock on Drea's door when it swung wide open. Drea took in my raised hand as I took in her red-rimmed eyes. She wasn't disheveled, but she was close to it.

"Come to knock me out?" Drea snorted and indicated to my still raised fist.

"Oh. No. I actually came to see if you were okay," I said and lowered my hand.

"Are you kidding? I'm just dandy. Here I am trying to convince myself that my life doesn't blow, and then my mother decides to get knocked up, which means I now have to deal with you forever," she seethed.

I had half a mind to walk away, but I decided to press on. She'd looked human at the table. That was the part of her I needed to get through to. "I know it's not ideal, and I'm not happy about it either. I just want to let you know that if you want to talk about it, I'm only a couple doors down."

"I am well aware of how close you sleep in proximity to me, Candace. I'm observant that way," she said.

"Okay, well I need to get ready for work, so have fun at your Dad's." I started walking down the hall.

"What the hell did you think was going to happen just there?" Drea called and stepped outside her door to lean against the wall.

"What?"

"What did you think was going to happen when you knocked on my door? I would fall into your arms, and we would cry together? Did you think I was going to forgive you for ruining my life and then trying to take it over?"

"I don't want your life," I shot back, regretting trying to be the bigger person. I should have let her cry alone in her room.

"You don't, huh? Could have fooled me. All those years you dressed like me and talked like me. I just thought you wanted to be my friend, but now here you are in my house, hanging out with my mother." When I didn't respond, Drea smile was triumphant. "This is my life and that, downstairs, is *my* mother, not yours. Your life got fucked the minute your father abandoned you, and then your mother abandoned you to get away for however long. Maybe you shouldn't be trying to comfort me when your life is in more pieces than mine. You're more broken than I am."

She retreated into her room for a moment and emerged with a designer duffle bag in her hand. She paused only to look at me as if she were going to say more, but then seemed to think better of it. Instead, she laughed and descended the stairs.

I stood in the hallway for a few moments before composing myself and changing for work. I'd gotten the soda stains out of my uniform. Little victories, right?

I wanted nothing more than to call Mom the moment I got into the car, but between the news of the baby and Drea's too-true words, I was barely holding it together. If I called her now, I wouldn't be able to make through my shift.

"There's our girl! See I told you there was no need to panic," Joe said, as I sped behind the counter to punch in. I shot them both a small smile, hoping I looked normal, and dashed into the break room to store my stuff.

When I emerged, Joe was right there. "I covered for you with Robby. I told him you had called and said you had car trouble, so if he asks that is your story. And this one," he said pointing to Mark, "was ready to send out a search party."

"I was not," Mark said quickly.

If I weren't so distracted by everything that had happened earlier, I probably would have given more thought to Mark's concern and his pink cheeks. Instead I said, "I'm here. No need to worry." Even I cringed when I heard how false my chipper voice sounded.

"Are you okay?" Joe asked. He moved even closer, getting ready to hug me.

I moved away from him quickly. Hugs in times like this made me cry. "Yep. I'm good. Just ready to get to work," I said and jumped onto one of the computers to help the customers in line. If I could focus on work, I could get through this night.

I was sure Joe thought I was out of earshot when he told Mark, "Now I know something is wrong. No one here is ever ready to get to work."

I had never been thankful for busy nights at work, but hey, there was a first time for everything. The lobby was packed enough that Joe couldn't get me alone to talk, which was for the best. The look on Dad's face when I brought up mom and the look on May's face when Drea had attacked her replayed in my mind as I took orders. I tried to focus on peppermint chocolates, instead of the shattered pieces of my life.

When it was time for my break, I tried to sneak into the break room to grab my coat and purse. I intended to take my break in my car away from other people, but I'd barely gotten my coat on when Mark came in.

"Hey. Going somewhere?" he asked. He gave me more space than Joe would have, and for that I was thankful.

"Yeah, I thought I'd go for a drive. Maybe swing through the Java Stop or something." I wrapped my scarf around my neck, hoping he would take the hint and let me be.

"So no studying tonight?" He held up his textbook.

"Oh shit. I forgot." My notes and textbook were on the desk in my bedroom.

"Hey," Mark said, reading my face, "it's not a big deal. We can worry about it all later. Besides, you've been acing quizzes lately. I doubt you need me anymore, and it's not like we've actually been studying recently anyway."

It was true. Our recent time together in the library and work had been filled with jokes and banter, almost as if we were friends, and I had been getting better grades in chem. My overall average had jumped since Mark had started helping me, and I was just about ready to send in my college applications. The deadline was January, so I still had just over a month and a half to get everything in order.

When Mr. Mason had handed back the first quiz I'd taken since Mark started tutoring me, he'd actually smiled at me. Elation had taken over me when I'd seen the "A" written boldly at the top of my paper. I hadn't realized I'd wrapped my arms around Mark in thanks until he'd tensed under my touch—and then hugged me back lightly. Lightning had shot through my body.

"Gross," Mindy had shot at us.

It had been her words that had sent a very startling reminder of where we were. I'd spent the rest of class trying to forget the way his hands felt, how my skin heated under his touch.

"If you don't want to study anymore, it's understandable," he said, bringing me back to the break room.

"No, no. It's not that I don't want to. It's just that I've got a lot of stuff going on, and I completely spaced it. It may sound strange, but I actually look forward to spending my break studying with you. God, that makes me sound so lame."

"Nah, it just means you like good company." He smiled. "Do you really want to leave for break?'

"I really just want to avoid Joe. I know he's going to try to find out what's going on. He's a great friend, but sometimes I just wish he couldn't read me so easily." I sighed and sat down on the only comfortable chair in the room.

"I have an idea. How about you just tell Robby you aren't feeling well, and we go to the best bookstore I know?" He must have seen the apprehension on my face because he quickly added, "Or you could just go home. No pressure to hang out with me." He raised his hands in the air like it wouldn't bother him either way.

"No, it's not that. It's just… I haven't seen your dad since your first night here."

"Don't worry about that. I told you he basically thinks you walk on water," he laughed.

I nodded, but still felt hesitant. Vincent may have convinced Mark to give me a shot, but I still felt awkward about seeing him now that he knew the truth about me.

"Look, I'm going to head over there, and if you decide to come too, that's great. If you decide you want to be alone, that's no problem either." He grabbed his coat and ball cap. His dark hair and eyes blended in with the bluish-black color of his jacket.

"Wait," I called as he reached the door, "how are you going to get off work? We can't both tell Robby we're sick."

"Actually, my shift ended about a minute after your break started."

I scrunched up my face in confusion. "Then why were you going to stay and study with me? It's Friday. You must have plans."

"We use our breaks to study, and I didn't want to let you down. Well, that and you looked like you could use somebody to talk to or sit with or something." He brought his hand to his head like he was going to run his hand through his hair, but forgot he had already put his hat on.

"You're a good guy, Mark," I said, catching us both off guard.

He nodded uncomfortably and left me alone in the break room. I spent a few minutes contemplating my options. I didn't want to stay and have the inevitable conversation with Joe, but I also wasn't sure about joining Mark. We hadn't spent time together outside of school or work, and I wasn't sure how it would go.

My pocket started to vibrate. I knew before I pulled my phone out that it was my mother. Most likely calling to check on me and assure me that she was "fine." I pushed the guilt away as I sent the call to voicemail. I would talk to her later, when I'd had time to process everything.

Joe peeked his head into the break room and moved to come in once he saw me. I knew if I let him start talking, I would never get out of here without spilling my guts, so I quickly stood and moved toward the door. He was my friend, but I'd go through him if I had to.

"Hey, I'm not feeling well. I'm going to go and tell Robby that I need to leave," I said, not slowing my pace toward the door. I hoped Joe would jump aside, but wasn't entirely surprised when he stood his ground, blocking my exit.

"You can tell Robby whatever you want, Candy dearest, but I'm not buying it." I opened my mouth to lie again, but he cut me off. "I get you're not in the mood to talk about it here. Too many eyes and ears and all that, but when you're ready to talk about it, I'm here." He wrapped his arms around me in a quick, supportive hug and moved aside so I could pass.

"Thanks, Joe," I said.

"Mhmm. Give Mark my best," he said.

I stopped. "How did you know?"

"Please. You're talking to the most observant male on the planet. He comes out of the break room with this weird look on his face, and I look in to see you in full deliberation mode. It's not rocket science." He rolled his eyes.

"It's not like that. He helps me study," I said a bit defensively.

Joe threw his head back and laughed. "Sure it is. I've seen that studying. Fitting that you're studying chemistry because the two of you do sure have a lot of it." He winked at me and left the room to get back to work.

I opened my mouth and then closed it. There was no use arguing with Joe when he had an idea in his head.

Robby wasn't happy with my departure, but he did let me leave without too much hassle. As if I didn't have enough to worry about, I now had thoughts of my supposed chemistry with Mark in my head, which was absurd. I'd be lucky if he actually called himself my friend. Still, when I walked through the door to the bookstore and watched Mark's face light up, I could feel my own lips pull up.

My nerves about seeing Vincent went out of my mind when he pulled me into an unexpected hug. "My dear! I thought you'd forgotten about me, or worse forgotten your love of books." He smiled.

"Never!" The smell of comfortable leather chairs and old books filled the air, and I felt instantly at ease. It was like a homecoming of sorts.

"I knew it," he said. "Mark tells me you're studying together. It's so nice to know he's making new friends. He has good friends of course, but one can never have too many good people in their lives." He held my shoulders as he spoke. It was as if I'd been away for years, instead of a couple weeks.

"Dad, you're smothering her," Mark said, rubbing the back of his neck.

At that, Vincent laughed and stepped back. "Well, I only get to see her for a minute." He turned to me and said apologetically, "I have a later dinner planned for nine. Who eats dinner this late, I will never know."

"When you're young and hip, nine doesn't seem too late, I suppose," I said.

"It's getting late, Dad. You don't want to be late," Mark urged.

"Okay, okay. I'll get going. Be sure to lock up when you leave, and get this girl some tea if she wants." He hugged Mark, who surprisingly didn't look embarrassed in the least by the show of affection, before exiting his shop with a final wave over his shoulder.

Mark was shaking his head when I turned to face him. He'd ditched his ball cap, which allowed me to see his eyes more. I decided I liked him better without the hat.

"What?" I said.

"He's more excited to see you than he is me. You should hear him when your name gets brought up."

"It's tough being universally loved," I said as seriously as I could.

Mark chuckled and waved me into the sitting area where there was a teapot already waiting with two cups around it.

"Were you that positive that I would come?" I asked.

"No, but I wanted to be ready in case you did."

I didn't know why, but I believed him. He wasn't cocky, like most guys my age were. He was just honest.

"These are beautiful." I picked up one of the delicate teacups. Black orchids stood out against the white ceramic. Black flowers usually looked gothic, but these were classic.

"My mom got them from her mom," he said and took the cup gently to pour the tea.

"So your dad has big plans tonight?" I took the cup Mark handed me and sat down.

"He told me he was meeting with an old friend," he said and used his fingers to do air quotations at the word *friend*. "I think he's afraid to use the actual word date in front of me." He took the chair next to me and poured his own cup of tea.

"Your parents aren't together?" For some reason, I didn't picture Vincent being divorced, but it occurred to me he'd never mentioned his wife before.

"My mom died when I was thirteen," he said. He kept his eyes on his tea as he spoke. After a beat, he looked at me, but I couldn't keep his gaze. I was so afraid I would look at him the way people looked at me when they found out about Austin. Like they expected to see my brokenness over the tragedy.

"I am so sorry. I didn't mean to bring it up," I said, trying to backtrack.

"It's okay, really. It's always weird when it comes up for the first time around people because they get that look of pity in their eyes, and I'm not a huge fan of that. But it comes with the territory."

I nodded. I didn't know what it was like to lose a parent, but I did know about loss.

"My dad doesn't want to admit that he's dating someone. I think he thinks I'll flip out or something, even though I've told him that I'm okay with it."

"Maybe he just wants to make sure you really believe that before he tells you," I suggested.

"Maybe," he said. "Don't get me wrong. I miss my mom everyday, but he shouldn't have to be alone forever." The cup he held looked small in his hands as he played with it.

"How did it happen, if you don't mind me asking?"

"Cancer. It was fast. We had time to say goodbye at least. When she was gone, we decided we needed to start fresh, so we moved to Brinkerville. Dad opened the store and now here we are." He lifted his hands and spread them wide.

"Makes sense. Although I have to tell you, most people make plans to move *out* of Brinkerville, not *in*." At the sight of Mark's confusion, I explained, "Kids are always moving away for college because they're over the small-town feel of things."

"Ah, I see. Is that your plan? Move away to a big city?"

"Not really. I'm hoping to get into Dartmouth."

"Really?" His eyebrows shot up.

I nodded and waited for his response. I briefly worried that it would be like Drea's, and he would laugh, thinking it was a joke.

"That's great! I'm actually applying there too. Well, I already sent my application in. Did you?"

"No, I'm thinking this week or next. I was really just waiting until my chemistry grade was solid." I took a sip of tea and relaxed a bit more into the chair.

He nodded and we fell into an elongated silence. It wasn't altogether uncomfortable, but Mark's fidgeting made me believe that he wasn't a huge fan of it.

"So," I said, "what do you normally do when you're not at school or working?"

"Want to know if I'm out raging at parties?" he asked, dryly.

"I guess you could put it that way," I said, rolling my eyes. "No, it's more that I'm curious. I never saw you here before the first night we worked together. I know you go to the movies sometimes, but everyone does that."

"Seems like you know a lot more about be than you let on." He smiled and then shrugged when I pinned him with a stare. "Mostly, I hang out with my friends Greg and Steve, and I'm not as embarrassed as I should be to admit that we do spend a good amount of time on my Xbox-One."

"Ah, the Xbox—the enemy of girlfriends everywhere."

"Well, mine wasn't fazed by it." Something unidentifiable sank inside me.

"But that's because she doesn't exist," Mark said and looked at me like he knew what I'd been thinking.

"I wouldn't be bothered if you did. I'd just feel sorry that she has to deal with you all the time."

He smiled. "Sure, whatever you need to tell yourself."

"What about Shannon? Don't you hang out with her a lot too?" I kept my face impassive.

"Actually, no. I mean we hang out a lot at school, but that night at the movies was a rarity. Shannon doesn't get to come out a lot. Her dad's kind of ..." He looked uncomfortably lost as he searched for the right word to describe Mr. Bowen.

"Strict," I supplied, but knew I was oversimplifying him.

He'd been a tense man when I'd known him. Ready to snap at any moment. I'd never seen it, but I'd felt it anytime I'd eaten dinner with the Bowens. His eyes darted around, like he'd been waiting for something to happen. For someone to make him angry.

I used to think maybe he was too intense. Mom thought the reason Mr. Bowen was so overprotective was because of how sick Shannon had been when we were younger. "If you were always sick like that, I would keep you inside the house forever," Mom had said. I'd let it go, mostly because Shannon had rarely spoken about her father when we'd been friends. Still, there was something about Mr. Bowen, something just below the surface, something dark. I'd felt it.

"I didn't know you two used to be friends until that night I came in for the job application, and I asked her about it. Then, you know, she told me what happened. Well, some of it I guess." He looked down at the floor.

"She told you what a bitch I was, you mean?" I played with my now-empty teacup, afraid to see judgment in his eyes.

"Actually, no. She never insulted you. Never name-called or things like that. She told me you used to be super close." He sounded as confused as I felt. The Shannon I remembered never trash-talked anyone, but I was amazed that time and high school politics hadn't changed her.

"She's a much better person than most," I said softly. Mark nodded in agreement.

As much as I felt almost compelled to find out more about Shannon, I felt bad using my time with Mark like this.

"What about you? What do you normally do?" he asked, like he, too, needed to get to redirect the conversation.

"Oh my life is very, very fascinating," I said. "Should I start with my favorite Netflix show?"

We stayed in the bookstore talking about nothing, and in some ways everything. As I sat there listening to him laugh or feeling his eyes on me while I answered a question, I was struck by the importance of the moment. It was the start of something. I didn't know what, but it was something new. We'd been together plenty times before, but not like this, not like we were friends.

"Tonight was nice," I told him when he locked the door to the bookstore.

"Yeah, it was fun hanging out with no studying or anything," he said. He stuck his hands in his pockets as he walked me to my car. I'd moved it to the parking lot in front of the store, but it was still sweet of him to walk me.

"It was a distraction I didn't know I needed," I said and my smile faded a bit as I thought about everything I would have to deal with at home at some point.

"You looked like you needed it when you came in," he agreed. "I'm happy I could help. Anytime you need a distraction, I'm your guy."

"What about when I need a friend?" I asked. We hadn't established if that was what we were, but it felt like the time to broach the subject.

He looked at me for a moment. His eyes searching mine, and I thought maybe I'd pushed it too far.

"I can be that too," he said. His eyes were still on me, and I felt a blaze of heat spread through me. The sudden urge to kiss him overwhelmed me, and my face reddened at the thought. He'd been kind enough to offer friendship, and I was ready to jump him. How pathetic was I?

I shook my head to clear the invading thoughts and got into my car with a last goodbye to him. Through my embarrassment, his face kept entering my mind on the ride home, and it was hard to forget the way his eyes had found my lips just before I'd gotten into the car.

CHAPTER 12

I woke the next morning to a buzzing from my nightstand. When my mother's name appeared on the caller ID, it occurred to me that I had never called her back last night, and the baby bombshell came tumbling back to me.

"Hello," I said groggily and cleared my throat.

"Morning, sunshine!" Mom's voice reminded me of the false-cheery ones game show hosts put on. "Did I wake you?"

"Yeah, I guess so."

"Oh. It's almost nine. I thought you'd be up by now." The cheery tone was replaced by concern.

"I didn't sleep well last night," I said. I'd tossed and turned more than usual. The last time I'd checked the clock it had been four in the morning.

"I can only imagine. Your father called last night to tell me he'd told you. I had hoped to get ahold and make sure you were okay."

I pulled the covers up to my chin, like my down cocoon could protect me from the truth. I had no idea what role I would play in the baby's life, and it made my head hurt to think about it for too long. It was hard to remember it wasn't the baby's fault dad was in the running for Worst Father of the Year.

"I'm okay. I think… Honestly, I have no idea what to feel. Are you okay?" I hated thinking of her dealing with this news all alone and so far away.

"I am," she answered with a calm tone. "I don't think it's ideal for your father or May, but it's done. There's no point in being upset. He's not my husband anymore."

Her composed voice surprised me. I was sure she would cry or at least throw a dig at dad, but she didn't. She was taking the news with class, and I felt a surge of love for her.

"I hate dad," I blurted. I meant to follow Mom's composed example, but I couldn't. It was all still too raw for me.

"Oh Candace, I know you think that, but you don't. Not really. Deep down, you love your father."

"He replaced us," I said, feeling childish.

"He couldn't replace you if he tried, which he never would. Your father does love you. And I can't believe I'm saying this, but it seems like he is struggling with the idea of a new baby as much as you are."

"He's replacing Austin," I whispered. "What am I supposed to do? Tell him that I'm happy this is happening?"

My mother's breathing was the only audible sound for a moment. "No, I don't think you need to go that far. I just think you need to remember that you don't hate your father. He meant too much to you before for you to hate him now."

"It feels like I hate him," I muttered.

"I know it does, sweetie," she said in a gentle tone.

A couple of voices called to her on the other end of the phone. Mom seemed to be holding the phone away from her mouth as she said, "I'll be right there." After a few moments of muffled conversation, my mother's attention was directed back to me. "Candace, I have to get back to a meeting. Please call me if you need me. I know this hasn't been easy, but I'll be home soon. I love you."

"I love you too." I wanted nothing more than to beg her to come home, but if she could be strong, then I could be too.

After hanging up with Mom, I had no idea what my next move was. I heard people moving around downstairs, but wasn't ready to face any of them. I was more than content to pull the covers back over my head and go back to sleep.

I had almost drifted off again when my phone buzzed. Part of me thought it was Mom again, but the text was from a number I didn't recognize.

"Hey. Do you have plans today? This is Mark btw." Joe gave me your number.

"I don't," I typed back quickly.

"Want to meet at the diner in 30?"

I heard a light knock on my door before it cracked open, revealing Dad on the other side. He looked as tired as I felt. Stubbles of graying hair were visible on his usually clean-shaven face.

Instead of acknowledging him, I took a moment to send a quick text to Mark saying that I'd be there soon.

"Can we talk?" he asked and took a hesitant step inside.

"Actually, I have to get ready," I said getting out of bed and heading toward my closet.

"Working again? This is too much, Candace," he said, annoyance heavy in his voice.

"Actually, I'm not working. I am going to meet a friend at the diner." I picked out a navy V-neck sweater and a pair of leggings. They would do.

"Which friend?"

"Just one from school," I said. I went into the bathroom to brush my hair and teeth and hoped Dad would take my avoidance as a sign that I didn't want to talk.

Unfortunately, he wasn't swayed and appeared in the doorway of the bathroom a few moments later. "I'm happy you're taking my advice and doing something other than working, but we need to talk. I know this news can't be easy for you, and I want us to work through it." He kept his tone formal, like we needed to work through a contract discrepancy.

I spat toothpaste into the sink and rinsed my mouth before I turned around to face him. "I get that you think we need to talk, and maybe we do. I'm just not ready to talk to you about this right now," I said, brushing past him. If I didn't stop moving, maybe he would leave me alone.

Dad stood there looking calculating and a bit helpless, and it reminded me of the day I'd moved in. We'd gotten nowhere in the time I'd lived here. We were still strangers. I gave him my best "don't do this to me right now" face, and he seemed to understand that this was something he just couldn't push.

He left my room with a nod and relief washed over me. But soon after, that feeling began to fade, and I was left feeling like a coward. I was too afraid of a serious conversation with him. It was easier to be angry with him than to forgive him and trust him again. I'd trusted him before, and he had failed me catastrophically.

By the time I pulled into the parking lot of the diner, I was officially ten minutes late. Cars cluttered the parking lot as they usually did on weekend mornings.

Mark was already seated at a booth in the far corner. When he spotted me, he offered me a relieved smile.

As I made my way toward him I noticed a few people from school in the booths on the near wall, and I offered them polite smiles without looking long enough to see if they smiled back.

It wasn't until I almost reached Mark that I saw Luke and his family. Luke noticed me a moment later, and his brows knitted in confusion. It had been a long time since I'd last come to the diner for Saturday morning breakfast with Luke and his family. I checked quickly to see if Drea was with him, and I was pleasantly surprised to see that she wasn't. Perhaps she wasn't home from her father's yet, and Mark and I could have a peaceful breakfast.

It wasn't lost on me that Luke watched me walk the rest of the way to Mark. I wondered briefly if his whole family was taking turns looking at me. I was sure they all hated me now, too. How could they not? Especially if he'd told them about what I'd supposedly done.

"Hi," I said as I sat down across from Mark.

He looked casual in jeans and a gray flannel. The darkness of the gray highlighted his dark eyes and hair. He had a cup of coffee and a muffin in front of him.

He looked down at the muffin and smiled. "I got a little hungry," he said sheepishly. "Do you want some?" He pushed the plate toward me, and I took a small piece off the top.

"Mmmmm. I forgot how good these are." I stole another piece.

"I got chocolate chip because I thought it was a safe choice."

"Chocolate chip is always a good choice. It was sweet of you to think of me."

He shrugged, but pinkness spread in his cheeks from my compliment.

I picked up the menu and perused it quickly. It was for show. I always got the same thing: huevos rancheros with extra jalapenos. It was the best wakeup on a Saturday morning. When I'd stopped coming here, I'd tried to make the dish with mom, but it never tasted quite right.

"*There's* a face I haven't seen in awhile," said Carly. She was a plumpish waitress who had been working here for what seemed like forever. Carly had waited on me when I'd come in with

Dad when I was little and later, when I'd come in with Luke's family. She looked the same as ever: hair tucked in a bun, her yellow uniform crisp and clean.

Carly gave me a quick pat on the shoulder. "Finally decided you missed me, huh?"

"Of course I did! How are things here? Still serving the best coffee in town?"

"You mean the only coffee in town," she laughed. Her voice had grown raspy over the years. "Things here are the same. Arnold's still working the kitchen and grumbling this and that, but you know him."

"Well it's good to hear some things never change." I smiled. Looking around, the diner looked just as I remembered it. Old black-and-white photos of sundaes and kids lined the walls, and the booths were still covered with the same worn leather.

"That it is. I see neither of you are sitting with your normal crowd," she said, letting her insinuation linger. Carly ate up gossip like it provided her sustenance. I couldn't help but wonder whom Mark usually came in with.

Neither of us replied to her. It was as if we were locked in a game of chess. When she realized she would get nothing from us, she huffed, "Fine. If you're not going to budge, do you both want your regulars?" She pouted like our silence put her out.

We both nodded. He had a normal crowd and a regular order?

"Could I also have green tea, please?" I asked.

Carly nodded as she walked away to put our order in.

"So you have a regular order?" I said directing my attention to Mark.

"I would love to say I'm special, but this town is small enough that anyone who comes in here more than once could be considered a regular," he said. He played with a straw wrapper on the table and looked at me. It was the only thing he did that let me know he was a bit nervous about our breakfast meeting.

I heard the familiar sound of Mrs. Jackson's laughter, and the oddness of the situation hit me. I used to laugh with her. I'd loved Mrs. Jackson. When I thought of Luke, my thoughts often drifted to his family, making me wonder if I missed them more than I actually missed him.

"We can go if you want." Mark looked from me to Luke and his family. His forehead was creased with concern, but his expression showed nothing but calm understanding.

"No, I want to stay. I'm just taking all the changes in." I tried to smile but knew it probably looked forced. I was here with Mark, and he didn't deserve to play second fiddle to the ghost of boyfriends past.

"If it makes you feel any better, he keeps looking over here when he thinks no one is watching." He didn't sound happy about it, but didn't say anything more.

"Probably wondering why I finally decided to come out of hibernation," I said.

Mark's gaze flicked back to me. "Why did you?" There was a certain intensity behind his calm façade that I hadn't seen before. As quickly as I saw it, it was gone.

"Um, I guess it was the right time, and of course the right person asked me." Had it been anyone else who asked me, my answer would have been no. I wasn't quite sure what that meant, and I wasn't sure I was ready to know. "So Mr. Regular, do you hang out here with Greg and Steve?"

"I don't think you have any room to make fun of me for being a regular when you have a regular order, too, but yeah, normally I come here with those two."

Carly brought over my tea, and I took a moment to add a bit of lemon. "Why aren't you here with them this morning, instead of me?"

His mouth quirked up. "I guess I find I like this company a bit more."

His deep tone caused that familiar fluttering in my stomach and chest. Even before Luke had broken up with me, the fluttering had stopped. We'd dated for years, and part of me rationalized that it was just what happened to couples over time, but sitting here in the booth with Mark, I knew my rationalization had been very, very wrong.

Carly arrived with our food moments later, and it wasn't until she went to place the plates on the table that I saw how close our hands were, almost as if we were reaching out for each other across the table.

I snatched my hand back quickly as Carly sent me a Cheshire smile. I was so busted.

"Good to see you with a boyfriend who looks at you like you shine bright," Carly gushed.

"Oh we're not … He's not…" I looked to Mark for help, but he seemed to enjoy the way I squirmed for words.

A curious smile spread across his lips and his dark eyes seemed to dance. When I glared at him, he laughed and said, "We aren't together."

Simple. Why couldn't I have just said that?

"Could have fooled me," she teased as she walked away.

Carly had been the second person to say something like that about us, and it made me wonder how we really looked to other people. If people looked at us now, would we look like a couple?

At a loss for what to say, I dug into the meal in front of me. The moment the first bits of egg and jalapeno touched my tongue, my eyes shut in delight. How had I gone this long without this?

"That good, huh?" Mark's voice broke into my thoughts.

I opened my eyes to find him smiling at me. "Amazing," I said. I pushed my plate toward him, inviting him to try for himself, but he eyed it doubtfully.

"I'm not a huge fan of spice," he said. I nudged my plate toward him again, not taking no for an answer, and he took a small piece of egg and salsa and popped it into his mouth. He moved his head from side to side as he assessed the taste of my breakfast. "That's actually pretty good," he conceded.

"I wouldn't steer you wrong."

Something caught Mark's eye from the entrance of the diner. Turning around, I saw two boys in fall jackets staring at us. "Remember when I told you I come here with Greg and Steve?"

I barely had time to nod before the boys were at our table. Both were red-faced from the cold outside.

"See, I told you he would be here," one of the boys said. "But I didn't expect him to have company. Replaced us, have you?" He had unruly brown hair and deep blue eyes—the kind people fell into. He wore his grin devilishly, and I had no doubt he used his good looks to his advantage. If I'd ever taken the time to notice him before, I couldn't say whether or not the smile would have worked on me.

"This is Greg and Steve," Mark said. He opened his mouth, I assumed to introduce me, but Steve sat down next to him, surprising everyone. Greg, the one with the smile, was a bit more polite, and only sat down when I motioned toward the seat next to me.

I extended my hand toward Greg. "I'm—"

Steve interrupted, "Candace Ellis. Believe me, we know." He looked at me coolly, like I had been the one to crash his breakfast plans.

I withdrew my hand quickly.

Greg shot him a look, but Steve didn't even look abashed. "What he meant to say was it's nice to meet you, Candace." Greg extended his hand like I had moments before and shook my hand firmly.

"You too," I said, thankful that Steve hadn't decided to interrupt our breakfast alone.

Greg turned to Mark and gave him a look of mock outrage. "If you had just told us you wanted prettier company, we wouldn't have stalked you."

"Speak for yourself. I'm the most gorgeous person I know," Steve said.

I let out a chuckle, but some of it stuck in my throat when Steve glared my way. Apparently we weren't on the laughing level. His eyes narrowed at me. "Think my looks are funny?"

"Not terribly," I answered honestly. With red hair and green eyes, he was kind of easy on the eyes, but his frown did little to brighten his face. I met his eyes and refused to look away. He wanted to intimidate me, but I'd seen scarier. Hell, I lived with scarier.

"Back off, Steve," Mark warned. He put down his fork and frowned at his friend.

Steve swung his gaze toward Mark in surprise, and darted his eyes back to me. "Sorry," he muttered.

"No problem," I said.

"Don't worry about Steve," Greg said, "he's just cranky because he sucks at *Rocket League.*"

"I told you, the buttons were sticking on my controller. It wasn't my fault."

"See, he's grumpy with everyone." Greg smiled as if his friend was helpless.

"You guys played this morning?" Mark asked. I could tell he felt left out, although his forlorn expression made me want to roll my eyes. I didn't get the appeal of videogames.

"Yeah, but don't worry, you didn't miss anything. I would have traded places with you in a second." Greg's devilish smile made another appearance. His eyes darted to Mark momentarily, so I suspected it was more to get a rise out of him than to actually make me swoon.

A moment later, Greg jumped beside me and let out a small yelp. But he kept his smile as he rubbed his shin.

"Are you guys eating?" Carly asked and placed cups of coffee in front of Steve and Greg. Both boys accepted their cups with grateful smiles. "Nah," Greg said, "we already ate. We just came in to bug Mark."

"I see. Let me know if you change your mind," she said and leaned over to refill Mark's cup before making the rounds to her other tables.

I pushed my plate away from me. More than half my meal still sat on it. It was delicious, but the portions were too big.

"You're done?" Steve eyed my plate with interest.

I debated eating the rest just to disappoint him, but reminded myself it wouldn't hurt to win over some of Mark's friends. "Yep. You want the rest?"

He pulled my plate toward him without hesitation. "Thanks," he said and bent his head down to shovel food in. His mouth sucked up food like a vacuum.

"Look at that! You found a way to the beast's heart." Mark put his napkin on his own plate. Steve looked up briefly to see if there was any food left on it and scowled when there wasn't.

"Dude, we just ate." Greg looked at his friend with mild revulsion.

Steve didn't respond until he had cleaned the plate. "I'm a growing boy. I need nutrients." He stared at it as if he were debating licking it clean.

"You're growing alright—in the stomach region." Greg reached forward to poke Steve's stomach, but Steve slapped his hand away indignantly. The three of us broke into laughter and after a moment, Steve joined in.

"What are your plans today?" Steve asked and nudged Mark with his elbow.

As the three boys discussed their possible plans, I was reminded that I was the outsider. They didn't once look at me to include me.

When the bill came, Mark insisted on paying for me. As we argued about it, I caught the significant glances between Steve and Greg. I wanted to tell them this wasn't whatever they thought it was, but didn't. In the end, Mark won, and I let him pay, but I had every intention of paying him back somehow.

I let the three boys walk ahead of me as we left. I hoped to say goodbye to Carly.

"Candace!" Mrs. Jackson called.

Uneasy, I looked to see where Mark was, but couldn't find him. Had he left without saying goodbye?

I made my way over to the Jacksons, and Mrs. Jackson pulled me into her chest. Her grip relaxed slightly when she felt the tension in my body at the surprise embrace. "It's so good to see you, dear."

"It's good to see you too, Mrs. Jackson."

"Brenda, please. You and Luke have been on a break for too long if you've reverted to calling me Mrs. Jackson," she laughed.

A break? Is that what he had told his family? How did he explain his relationship with Drea if he had told them we were on a break?

"Sorry," I said. I glanced at Luke, but his face betrayed nothing. He merely looked from his mother to me, careful to avoid direct eye contact.

"We have to get lunch soon. It's been dreadfully hard keeping up with the trends without my favorite girl."

I doubted that. Brenda Jackson was the most stylish mother I knew. Even now, she stood in knee-length boots, leggings, and an oversized sweater. On most people, it would look like they were swimming in a sweater like that, but Brenda pulled it off effortlessly.

"I would love that," I said with a smile, but a tightness began in my chest. Lunch was a line I couldn't cross.

"Fantastic. How's everything? Luke tells me your mother is out of town and you're staying with your father."

I paused, stunned that Luke had told his mother anything about me at all. "Yes, she'll be home soonish. I honestly can't wait to see her."

She made a small, sympathetic noise. "I can imagine. Well, at least you're able to have a friend close by. You know that girl you hang around with."

I briefly wondered why she hadn't just used Drea's name. "Actually, you all probably see Drea much more than I do. We have pretty busy schedules."

Behind his mother, Luke shifted uncomfortably in his chair.

"Why would we see Drea?" Her face showed genuine confusion that must have mirrored my own. Why *wouldn't* they see Drea if she was Luke's girlfriend?

Luke abruptly stood up and said, "Don't you have to work, Candace?"

"I do," I said, even though I didn't.

"Oh, okay. It was so good to see you," Brenda said. "Luke, walk her to her car."

To my surprise, Luke didn't argue. Brenda smiled at me and gave me one last hug. There was a lot of feeling in the hug, like she believed Luke and I were going to work through our issues.

Luke and I walked side-by-side, drawing looks from a few of our classmates. It was such an odd feeling to be stared at like that. They were probably wondering why Luke and I were in such close proximity to each other.

We walked through a set of doors into the entryway of the diner. It was empty. People were huddled inside the second set of doors to escape the almost winter chill. I stopped walking and turned to him. It was the first time we'd been alone since he'd broken in through my bedroom window.

"Your family seems like they're doing well," I said. I needed to tip toed into conversation slowly, like wading into the Atlantic Ocean in late May.

"They are." His voice had a cautious edge to it. He looked anywhere but at me.

"I miss them." I didn't know why I'd told him that. Why I'd showed vulnerability.

He let out a breath. "They miss you too," he admitted, though it was clear he didn't want to.

It was a small admission I didn't know I'd needed. Fear that Drea had so easily stepped into the role I'd filled for so long had eaten at me since I'd first seen them together.

"Luke," I said, and waited for him to look at me. When he did, it was like I was the most dangerous thing he had ever seen. He, or a part of him, was afraid of me. "Why doesn't your family know about Drea?"

He shook his head like he wasn't going to answer. His mouth went taut like it did when he was in pain, like when his grandfather had died. I'd watched him shut down then. "I didn't tell my parents why we broke up. I didn't even tell them *that* we broke up. I told them it was a break."

Break. There was that word again. "Why would you do that?"

"I wasn't going to say anything at all, but my mother was relentless. I just… I couldn't tell her the whole story." He shoved his hands in his pockets like he always did when he was uncomfortable. It was strange how well I still knew his body language. "When Drea and I started fooling around, I didn't take it seriously. And … well, you know my mom isn't the biggest fan of girls like Drea."

Biggest fan was putting it lightly. Brenda Jackson made no secret of disliking Drea. She had once called her "callous and shallow" when Luke had hosted a movie night.

"She liked *me* okay, and I used to be a lot like Drea."

"No, you weren't. You weren't exactly likable when you were around her, but when you were on your own; you were easy going, easily loveable. You laughed at all the dumb jokes my dad told. You hung out with my mom because you actually wanted to. Do you think Drea would ever do that?"

I shook my head immediately, needing no time to think about my answer. There was no way Drea ever would. She thought Brenda was tacky and lame, and she hated puns. Maybe I hadn't been replaced after all. I didn't realize I was smiling until Luke's expression lost all hints of softness. "I said you *were* lovable, not that you are."

Ouch.

"For a moment, I thought you weren't going to be rude. I thought maybe we could talk civilly, especially since your puppet master isn't here."

He pointed at me. His finger too close to my face. "Don't try to act like you're in this position because of Drea. You did what you did, and now you have to lie in the mess you made. Any hope of us having a civil conversation flew out the window when we broke up."

"You broke up with me! You broke my heart, not the other way around." I tried to contain my anger, tried to remind myself that people in the diner would be able to hear us if we got too loud.

"You cheated." His trump card.

I let out a harsh laugh that made him step back. "I told you the day you accused me and I'm telling you now: I never cheated on you." When his mouth went into a taught line again, something clicked in my head. "You know what I think? I think you don't really believe I did anymore, either. You would have told your family if you really thought I'd cheated, but you didn't. You just don't want to look weak by admitting it. You wouldn't be keeping Drea a secret from your family if you really believed I cheated. What happened, Luke? Did she let slip she lied to everyone, or did you finally wise up and realize Drea was a born liar?"

"Shut up!" he roared and it was almost enough to make me step back.

"Why, so you can fool yourself some more?" My breathing was coming out hard, and it felt like every ounce of my anger and resentment buried from the last months was coming out of every pore of my body. I wanted him to hurt, like he'd hurt me. I didn't know what that said about my character, but in this moment I didn't care. I was tired of being the only one hurting. There was something cathartic about finally releasing my anger.

Anger permeated the air as we both stood tensely in the entryway. Luke extended one hand toward me—to kiss me or shake me, I wasn't sure which. I wanted to step back, but I was rooted to the spot. The door to the outside opened, and Luke jerked back from me.

Steve stood in the doorway, judgment clear on his face.

Guilt burned through me. Our position was innocent, but what was going on between Luke and me somehow wasn't. Luke's back slowly released some of the tension, and he stepped back through the diner doors without a word to either of us, or a second glance at me.

"We waited for you. I told them I'd come get you." He stepped into the entryway fully, letting the door shut behind him.

"You found me," I said weakly, coming down from my anger and whatever else I'd felt when Luke had been near me.

"That I did," he said curtly. His arms crossed over his chest like a bouncer.

"Is there a reason you hate me?" I blurted.

He stared at me for a moment as if he wasn't sure I was worth his next words. "I don't trust you. It's not hard to see that you miss your old life." He nodded toward Luke. "Mark likes you, and I don't want you to fuck with his head."

"I'm not trying to fuck with him." My voice was soft.

"Doesn't matter. You want your old life back, that's fine. But tell me, would Mark have a place if things went back to how they were?"

The question caught me by surprise. I missed my old life more often than I should. I missed not having people whisper about me when I walked by, and I missed having friends, if that was what they even were. I would be a liar if I said I hadn't fanaticized about it.

"I'm pretty sure my life is never going back to what it was, so you don't have anything to worry about."

His frown deepened. "See that's the wrong thing to say. You should want Mark in your life no matter if you're popular or a pariah, and until you know what you want, you're just going to fuck with him. He's a good friend. Good enough to try to be yours," he said and then added, "They're waiting for us."

He had the kindness to hold the door open for me as we left the diner, and I hated him for it.

When I went outside, Steve got into Greg's car and Mark waited outside of mine. He leaned causally on my hood. He hadn't left me after all, and that made me feel all the worse. "Sorry. I didn't realize you were waiting," I said.

"No worries," he said. "The guys want to know if we want to head over to Greg's house. I can teach you how to play some games if that interests you at all. If not, we can find something else to do."

I couldn't help but focus on his use of the word *we*. Somewhere in the time we'd spent together, we'd become a type of *we,* and I wasn't sure how to feel about it. My residual anger from the conversation with Luke told me I wasn't ready for the coupley definition. I might hate Luke, but that hate proved I wasn't completely over him. If I carried on this road with Mark, we would become something more. I could feel that in my gut, and I knew how much damage could be done if I entered into something with him too soon. Having Steve's words play in my head oddly made things easier for me.

"That's okay. I've already taken up too much of your time today." I tried to keep my voice light. "Thanks again for breakfast," I said and threw myself in the car. I turned the engine over and made to put it in reverse, but Mark jumped in the passenger seat before I could.

"What are you doing?" I sputtered, amazed at how fast he'd moved.

"Trying to figure out why you're blowing me off." The look on his face was one of hurt and confusion, and I cursed myself for being responsible for putting it there.

"I'm not blowing you off." Yes, I was, and I hated it.

"Really? Because that, out there, felt like a blow-off. Did I do something to offend you?"

"No, nothing like that." I pushed my hand against my forehead in frustration.

"What's it like then?" I had to hand it to him. He was determined. "Does this have to do anything with your conversation with Luke?"

I grimaced. "You saw that?"

"I thought about coming in to see if you were okay, but you're tough, so I knew you could handle it."

"You think a lot more of me than I actually am," I whispered.

"I think you just need to see how great you are."

I smiled at him, strangely thankful he had jumped in the car, but I still felt I had to be careful with his heart. "You're a good friend."

"The blatant friend card. That hurts a little." He grabbed his chest like I had wounded him, but he kept his easy smile.

"You're the first friend I've made in a long time, and I don't want to do anything to jeopardize that." I gripped the steering wheel and waited for the verdict. Mark was a really good person, but what if he didn't like me calling the shots? Would he leave me behind like almost everyone else?

"I told you last night, I can be your friend," he said.

"Thank you," I breathed and relaxed for the first time since my conversation with Luke.

"Of course. Now are you down to hang out today? Because I could teach you everything you need to know to kick Steve's ass in any video game of your choosing."

He flashed me a smile as he waited for my answer. His eyes were friendly, but there was still something more behind them; I just didn't know what. I'd just drawn the line, but as I sat there with him, I felt the temptation to cross it. "I'm game."

CHAPTER 13

It was a Saturday night, and I wasn't working, which was pretty amazing. And I wasn't alone in my room, binge-watching anything, which was also amazing. I was the poster child for progress.

I'd spent the entire day with Greg, Steve, and Mark. They'd welcomed me, not quite with open arms in Steve's case, and made me feel like I was their friend, not just Mark's.

When they'd invited me along on their adventure this evening, I had been skeptical. I'd never been to Go-Go's. Located about fifteen miles outside of town, it was the place for things like batting cages and go-kart racing. I'd heard about it when it had opened up a few years back, but my friends had never seemed interested in it. Luke and his friends had gone once or twice, but definitely not on a Saturday night, which had been reserved for drinking in Mindy's or Drew's basements.

Despite my hesitation, I felt the excitement spark as we got out of the car. I'd never actually been in a batting cage, and I was more than a little nervous about objects flying toward my face. The guys were most excited about the racetrack.

When we went into the building, the boys wasted no time heading toward the sound of rumbling tires. The large lights illuminated the track clearly. It was smart to build one of them inside, as summers in New England were so brief.

I kept pace with them, but craned my head to get a good look inside the various rooms in the building. Children ran excitedly from game to game. My parents had never done this kind of stuff with Austin and me, but after watching the tired looks on the parents' faces in here, I really couldn't hold it against them.

Mark held a wristband out to me. "This gets us unlimited rides. Steve's brother works here, and he hooks us up."

"That's convenient," I said as Mark wrapped the wristband around me.

The noise around the track was loud enough that people had to raise their voices to be heard over one another. Some chose to add elaborate hand gestures to make up for the loudness of the track.

As we got in line, Steve rocked back on his heals and eyed the karts on the track as they sped past. The look of determination and concentration in his eyes made me feel like I was missing something important.

I looked at Mark to see if he was watching the track the same way, but found his eyes on me. "What?" I asked a bit self-consciously.

"Just wondering why you look so confused." He smiled at me, but there was a touch of concern in his face as well.

"Oh, I'm just wondering how seriously you guys take this." I nodded toward Steve, who still looked, undeterred, at the track.

Mark let out a snort. "You mean how seriously *Steve* takes it. He hates to lose, so he gets super competitive with things like this. Unfortunately, he wins almost every time, and he's convinced that there's always one kart that's faster than the others, so he watches them while we're in line."

We shuffled forward in line as the people before us were allowed through the gate. We were next up, and I got as close as I could to watch people situate themselves in the karts.

"You ready? It's almost our turn." Greg nudged me as the karts took off, leaving only squealing in their wake.

"I think so," I said. I felt at ease standing with the three of them. It felt nice to be included again, welcome even. When I'd been out with Drea, Mindy, and Allison, I was always on my guard; it had been exhausting. It felt good to stand next to people who had no expectations of me, except to just be there with them.

"Have you ever ridden a go-kart before?" Mark asked.

"Can't say that I have," I admitted.

At that, Steve took his eyes off the track. He looked mildly horrified at my inexperience. "Just because you're new doesn't mean I'm going easy on you."

"I wouldn't expect you to," I shot back, a bit more fiercely than I meant to. Steve hadn't exactly softened toward me, but I would go so far as to say that he tolerated my presence.

We watched as the drivers all passed the finish line and pulled the karts in. They looked windswept as they got awkwardly out of the them. I was struck by how happy they were. Like they were all having the time of their lives. Had I ever looked like that with Drea?

As we walked onto the track, Steve ran ahead to pick the kart he had scouted before. I could feel myself getting swept up into his excitement and had a strong desire to win. The kart wasn't easy to get into, and I felt that there was no real way to not feel awkward while I adjusted myself behind the wheel.

As the attendant was coming around checking the seatbelts, I felt a slight bump from behind me. I twisted around to see Mark grinning innocently.

"Please remember there is a rule against bumping into other karts," the attendant said pointedly to Mark.

I didn't turn around to look at Mark, but I heard him call over an apology. The moment the attendant turned his back, I felt my kart jolt forward again.

The stoplights in front of us began their countdown. Steve gripped his steering wheel tighter, and I imitated him, my knuckles going almost white. When the light turned green, I slammed my foot down on the gas with all my might. My back slammed back into the seat as I took off and narrowly missed hitting Greg, whose cart, it seemed, didn't have quite the startup that mine did.

My hair flew wildly around my face as I sped toward Steve's kart, trying to catch him. My hands gripped the wheel harder as I rounded curves.

Out of the corner of my eye, I spied Mark closing in on the inside corner. As he got closer, he shouted, "Coming in hot!"

I didn't know how he had caught up to me so fast, but I had no intention of letting him pass. I waited for him to try to take the inside on a corner and closed him out. He bumped my tail end, accidentally this time, and jerked his wheel to avoid the wall next to them.

"No bumping," I called over my shoulder, with a wide smile he couldn't see.

Steve wasn't that far ahead. I wasn't sure why I wanted to beat him so badly. Maybe it was because he hadn't exactly been nice. Maybe it was because I wasn't good at losing either. No matter the reason, I felt the adrenaline kick in as I closed in on him.

He was so entranced in his own race that he didn't notice me until I pulled up beside him. I took the inside corner just like Mark had, except I was ready for Steve to try to box me out and gave him a slight bump to beat him to it.

"Hey!" he yelled as I sped by.

I raised one hand to wave at him and laughed wildly. I crossed the finish line first with Steve right behind me. Mark and Greg pulled in just a few moments later.

The moment I was out of the kart, Mark was by my side. "Who knew you had such great driving skills."

We walked toward the exit and caught up with Steve and Greg. Steve was waving his hands wildly, and I was pretty sure it was because I'd beat him. As we walked up to the two, Greg patted Steve on the shoulder good-naturedly.

Greg slung his arm around me and congratulated me on my win. "You dethroned the champ!"

Steve scowled at me. "There's no way that was your first time."

I held up my hands. "I swear I've never driven one before. Just a natural I guess." It was poor sportsmanship, but I loved winning.

Mark laughed. "And she is so modest."

"Whatever," Steve said sourly. "Best of three?" Steve held the gate open for us to exit and fell in next to me while he waited for me to accept or refuse his challenge.

"Sounds good to me."

We hopped back in line, and Steve and Greg discussed strategy. Mark and I hung back a bit. We stood close enough that our hands brushed once. Mark left his hands by his sides, but I moved mine to the pockets of my fleece even though they felt unnaturally warm from the contact.

"Do you think he'll forgive me?" I asked, nodding toward Steve.

"He'll forgive you the moment he beats you, but don't let his competitiveness fool you, he's impressed that you beat him. Thank you, by the way. Greg and I have to deal with him gloating every time we leave here."

"You guys are quite the trio."

"We're a pretty solid group, I guess," he conceded. "You've really never driven one of those before?"

"Nope. I'm ashamed to admit that I used to spend my weekend nights stealing bits of my parents' liquor and drinking with my friends. But that was before…" I stopped and shook my head to clear the memories. They were a bit fuzzy now, but still sharp enough to remember how high-pitched Mindy's voice had gotten as she drank, how Drew had staggered after four beers, how Luke had held me even closer—as if the drinks made him love me more.

"Do you miss it?" he asked.

Did I? If he had asked me months ago, my answer would have been an immediate yes, but standing here, feeling windswept and high on adrenaline with three people who expected nothing from me, I didn't think anything could be better.

"No," I said finally, "this is a good place to be."

"I think so too," Mark said and smiled.

I had no clue what my former friends were up to. I could have guessed based on my time with them, but for the first Saturday in a long time, I found I didn't care.

"We're up. You ready, Candace?" Steve's words had a challenge in them.

Oh, I was more than ready.

CHAPTER 14

The whispers as I walked by my classmates were the first clue that something was up. I tried to inconspicuously check out my outfit. My sweater and jeans appeared fine, but that gave me little comfort. It just meant that everyone around me knew something I didn't. It wasn't the first time I'd walked into school to something like this, but it never got any easier to be the one who had no idea what was going on.

I opened my locker, ready for some surprise, but there was nothing there. I tried to shake off the feeling of impending doom.

"Good morning," Mark said and I jumped. "Whoa, sorry I didn't mean to scare you. I thought you saw me."

I shut my locker and leaned back against it. "I didn't," I said irritably. When he frowned, I added, "I'm just feeling a bit watched this morning."

Mark looked around at the other students in the hallway. Most looked away when he looked at them, but some just kept on staring. "Oh, that's nothing to worry about."

"Really?"

"Nope, you just missed the memo. I became extremely popular overnight, so people want to get the gossip on my now popular-by-association friends." He smiled broadly and turned to our audience. "Autographs will be given free of charge," he said, cupping his hands around his mouth, so people in the hallway could hear him clearly.

Some took it as a sign to move along to their classes, but some just averted their eyes, pretending to look at their phones.

I smiled in spite of my nervousness. "I should have known you were destined for greatness. Do you think we can still be partners in chem?"

"Well, I've had a lot of offers, but I don't believe in abandoning the people who helped me reach the top."

We walked to class together, and while people still stared, I didn't mind it as much. Mark had a way of making whatever was going on seem insignificant.

I managed to almost block everyone else out entirely by the start of lunch.

I was washing my hands in the girls' bathroom when they came in. Allison blocked the door. To prevent me from leaving or prevent anyone else from coming in I wasn't sure, but either way, I was in trouble.

I reached for paper towels and tried to keep my hands from shaking. My plan was to ignore them entirely in the hopes that if I did, I could get out unscathed.

Unfortunately, Drea wasn't to be ignored. She moved toward me until her face was just inches from mine. "Have a nice breakfast at the diner?" she snarled.

"Breakfast?" I asked, not understanding why she cared about my breakfast with Mark.

"Don't play dumb," she spat and stepped even closer. Our noses were close to touching. "Everyone saw you flirting with Luke. Are you that desperate that you tried to get him back while I was at my father's?"

Her chest bumped mine forcefully and unexpectedly, causing my back to hit the wall behind me. I managed to keep my head from cracking against the wall. Anger bubbled in my gut. When I regained my balance, I shoved Drea with all the strength I had; she didn't even have time to stop me. There was no wall to catch Drea, and she fell backward to the ground. The four of us froze for a few moments. All of them just as surprised at what I'd done as I was. Drea's look was thunderous as she picked herself up. Mindy moved forward to help her, but Drea waved her off.

"Do you understand what I will do to you?" she seethed, although some of the effect was lost as she rubbed her backside.

"I mean, I guess. Problem is, you already took everything from me. I've got nothing left to lose."

Not entirely true, but I was more than willing to put out false confidence if it meant I could prevent Drea from kicking my ass.

"We'll see," she threatened and turned from me.

As Drea turned, I made the mistake of relaxing. She turned back as quickly as a snake and struck me hard across the face. Shock reverberated through my body as a metallic taste filled my mouth. My tongue flicked out to feel where my lip had split. I brought my hand up to my face, but dropped it when I saw Drea's look of satisfaction.

"Things can get worse for you—much worse," she said, and motioned to Allison to open the door.

On her way out, Mindy blew me a kiss.

I swallowed the lump in my throat and went to the mirror to inspect the damage. My lip was bleeding and the area around it was as reddening quickly. I searched my bag for something to cover the damage, but it was useless. I'd taken my makeup out months ago when I realized it was just taking up space.

I took a few calming breaths and assessed my next move. The redness would die down eventually, but I couldn't let anyone see me right now. Maybe I could make it to the deserted library unseen and give my face a chance to calm down. Peeking out of the bathroom, I didn't see anyone in the hallway and tried to move quickly and quietly toward the library. I didn't plan on Mr. Chagnon coming out of his room as I walked by.

Cursing under my breath, I tried to lower my head before he saw my face, but he wasn't as slow as some of the other teachers.

"Miss Ellis, who did that?"

"No one. I just had a bit of an accident," I mumbled, trying to move my lips as little as possible.

He looked at me like I had disappointed him somehow. He brought his hand to his shiny head and let out a grunt. "Follow me," he said and waved me onward.

Hoping he was taking me to the nurse for some ice, I was disappointed to find he was leading me to the guidance department. I cringed when he called Ms. Weatherbee out of her office. When she emerged, she looked from him to me and paused to take in my face.

"Miss Ellis seems to have had an accident," he said gruffly.

"I'll take it from here," she said to him and motioned for me follow her inside.

Her long, flowing skirt led me to a cushioned chair. It was difficult not to sneer at the inspiration posters lining her walls. "Stand up to bullies" and "Be THE hero" were the two biggest eye rollers. Whoever had made those knew nothing about high school.

Ms. Weatherbee went around her desk and sat down, so she was eye level with me. She tucked her graying hair behind her ears as she got a pen and notepad out. "Has there been some sort of altercation?" she asked. Her bracelets jingled as she readied her pen.

"I just ran into a door." Internally, I rolled my eyes. Even to me it sounded like a terrible excuse.

Ms. Weatherbee was silent for a second and then put the pen down. "I've had a lot of clumsy students run into things over the years. Doors, walls, chairs. Most of the time they had help running into those things."

I struggled to maintain eye contact. Her gray eyes were slightly hypnotizing.

"Well, I didn't have any help. I just can't seem to walk lately. I'm already embarrassed enough without getting dragged down here. People are already going to gossip about the state of my face without the added attention of having to talk to the school counselor."

I hoped I sounded just the right amount of outraged and embarrassed so Ms. Weatherbee would cut me some slack. It wasn't that my feelings weren't real, it was just that I had turned up the dramatics a bit.

Turned out, I was a better actress than I thought because Ms. Weatherbee's piercing look became sympathetic. "High school is hard enough without the added attention. Are your parents home? I could call them to dismiss you, that way you can head home."

Score. "My dad's working, but he has his cell. I drive myself to school, so I could drive home." Hope crept into my chest. If I could get home, I could avoid Drea and everyone else for a while.

"I'll give him a call. I'll be right back, okay?" Ms. Weatherbee's skirt bustled as she left the room.

I almost felt sorry for how easily Ms. Weatherbee was manipulated, but when she came in a few minutes later with my dismissal pass, it was all I could do to not do a little jig. One day for swelling to go down. Ice would be required. Now if only ice could take away Drea's swelling hatred for me.

***

I spent the rest of the afternoon on the couch, watching trashy daytime talk shows. By the second hour of it, I could see why people watched them religiously. It was like watching the downfall of the human race. My face was still sore, but I'd been icing it on and off. I could probably conceal it tomorrow.

Dad called to check on me, but it was easy to convince him that I was fine on my own at home.

When the doorbell rang, I didn't move to answer it. May had packages delivered all the time. Thanksgiving was approaching, so she'd ordered a bunch of things she thought she needed for it. The house was a revolving door of mailmen and packages. Normally, they just left them on the front porch after ringing the doorbell once. As it was, I was wrapped in a fleece blanket in a perfectly comfortable position and had little inclination to move. But the third time it rang, I threw the television remote aside and shuffled to the door, cursing May for her online shopping obsession. Who needed ten-plus crystal punch bowls?

When I opened the door not to a man in brown uniform but Mark, I debated if I could gracefully dash upstairs and change out of my old gray sweatpants into something a bit more flattering.

"Um, hi." I brought the door to rest in front of me, hoping to shield some of my lazy-day outfit.

Mark stood there, in his dark jacket with a few books and papers in his hand, looking the most unsure I'd ever seen him. "Hey! You weren't in our afternoon class, so I brought you the homework." He held it all up in case I hadn't seen. His uneasiness somehow eased mine, and I opened the door a bit more.

His eyes darted to my mouth a few times, and I could see he was trying—and failing—to avoid looking at it.

"How did you know where I lived?"

"I asked around… If this is weird, I can go," he said and made to leave.

"No! Come in, please." I waved him inside. When I shut the door, I added, "Stalking is illegal, you know."

The awkwardness broke apart and he smiled a familiar smile. The one that made my whole body heat. "Only if you report me, and if you want your assignments from today, I would suggest that you don't."

I smiled, but didn't laugh. The movement of my lip hurt, and I reached up to touch it, as if that could somehow relieve the pain.

"Drea did that," he said flatly and didn't bother to pretend he wasn't staring. He paused taking off his jacket momentarily as he took in my grimace.

"Yeah."

"Did you report her?"

"There's no point. If I did, it would just get worse."

Mark had a very clear thought process on what was right and wrong, but he didn't understand the extent Drea would go to if I said anything.

"She can't just assault people. You can't let her get away with it," he argued, and I felt my temper rise.

"I don't have to do anything. If you came here to tell me what to do, you know the way out." I crossed my arms to keep my hands from reaching up to touch my lip, which had started to ache ferociously.

He softened at the force of my words. "I'm sorry. It's just that she's terrible and she's only in high school. Imagine what kind of adult she'll be."

The thought of Drea as an adult, in some type of power position, scared the hell out of me. In ninth grade, the school guidance counselors came in to talk to us about bullying. Statistically, bullies didn't get what they deserved; instead, they grew up and became bigger bullies. An adult Drea would be a nightmare.

"I don't want to talk about her." I'd had enough of Drea for today and for a lifetime.

"Okay," he agreed and fought back a smile as he looked around at the ostentatious lobby. "I really did bring the homework from English. We got a poetry project." He handed me a few of the papers he had in his hand.

The missed work didn't look too bad, and I didn't think it would take me that long. I debated having us sit in the living room, but thought better of it. My room was the only place in the whole house that felt even remotely safe.

Thankfully, I'd done laundry the night before, so my clothes weren't scattered on the floor like they normally were. I shut the door behind us and gestured toward the desk in the corner, but Mark was more interested in inspecting my room. He reminded me of a detective searching for clues. I felt compelled to explain this wasn't my *real* room, but decided against it. Part of me wondered what he would make of it.

He stopped at the photo on my bedside table and picked it up. "Who is this?" he asked, pointing to Austin.

"That's my brother," I said. I loved that photo. We'd been at the beach and Austin had picked me up to swing me around. Dad caught the perfect moment of us both laughing without a care in the world.

I pulled the armchair over, so we could both sit comfortably in front of my laptop.

"I didn't know you had a brother." He replaced the photo and came to where I sat at the desk. He took the seat next to me and put the books and papers onto the dark wood.

"Austin," I said, playing with the frayed end of my t-shirt.

"He looks older. Is he in college?"

"He was. He died in a car accident two years ago." I kept my eyes trained on the dark mahogany in front of me. It never got easier to say this to people. It was the same wound sliced open every time.

"I'm sorry," he whispered. "I shouldn't have pried." He laid his hand upon my shoulder and squeezed gently.

"It's okay. We avoid talking about him. Maybe avoid is the wrong word, but after he died…It hurts to talk about him, but I like to sometimes."

Hesitantly, Mark asked, "What was he like?"

I looked at him and saw sympathy and open curiosity in his eyes. Coming from anyone else, it might have seemed like they were prying, but he was just giving me the opportunity to talk if I wanted. I wondered how he had gotten so good at interacting with others. Good enough to know just what I needed.

"He was…He was like the sun. That sounds so cliché, but everyone wanted to be around him. It's hard to explain, but people were just drawn to him. He was three years older than me, but he always made time to hang out with me. My parents argued a lot when we were younger, and he used to call me into his room and turn the TV up to drown out the noise." I felt my lips pull up and remembered how his arm had draped around my shoulders as he'd protected me. "When he died, everything just fell a part. My dad couldn't be in the house for extended periods of time and my mother couldn't stop crying. I…just felt confused. I didn't understand how the world could keep spinning if he wasn't in it anymore."

Mark moved his hand to hold mine. It wasn't a romantic gesture. It was just a way to show support if I needed it, and I normally did when I talked about Austin. I gripped his hand back.

"You don't ever talk about him. Like with your dad or anyone?"

"My dad and I don't talk about much anymore. He's having a new baby, so I'm not sure he even wants to."

"How do you feel about your dad having another child?"

"I don't know. It feels weird, but a part of me hates the kid already, and it hasn't even done a thing wrong. Does that make me a horrible person?"

Mark shook his head. "No. I think it just makes you human."

"Sometimes, with everything going on, human is the last thing I feel like."

I didn't cry exactly, but I didn't feel strong enough to talk either. Mark didn't say anything. He just held my hand and squeezed every few minutes to let me know he was there.

"Drea was there for me," I said and Mark's eyes widened. "She stayed at my house for a week and took care of me. Of all of us, really."

"I'm having a hard time picturing Drea doing that. She seems as caring as a viper."

I chuckled sadly. "She's not exactly warm and fuzzy, but she became exactly what I needed her to be after the accident. She took Austin's death hard too. They'd been close in a way… She saved me. Part of me, almost all of me, hates her now, but there will always be that little piece that's thankful. That will always remember."

"That makes sense," he said as he nodded his head. "She's still a walking nightmare," he added after a minute, like he couldn't help it.

I smiled lightly. Drea was a nightmare, but I'd seen the other side. That's what had made the crumbling of our friendship so much harder.

"What did I miss today at school?" I asked.

Mark didn't comment on the changing of the subject as he walked me through what I'd missed in English. He'd grabbed me an extra copy of the poetry assignment. It seemed simple enough.

"The best poetry comes from experience," I said. "You just pick a feeling, a moment, a symbol or something like that. I usually do webs to help me. I'll think of a moment and write down a bunch of adjectives or feelings associated with it, and then I'll start crafting a piece."

"You make it sound so easy," he said, glaring at the assignment sheet.

I shook my head. "It's not. I've just been practicing it for a while, so I have a technique that usually works for me. It's also easier after watching someone like Sarah Kay on YouTube. She's inspiring."

"Who?"

"You've never seen Sarah Kay?" When he shook his head, I grabbed my laptop. "You are in for a treat."

When I pulled up the first video, Mark drummed his fingers on the desk as if showing his lack of interest, but by the time the video was halfway through, the drumming had stopped, and I knew I had him. We stayed like that for the next hour or so, and every now and then I snuck a peek at him. His eyes were focused and sometimes his lips parted like he was going to recite what he'd heard.

We sat close together, our shoulders touching. I felt the strongest urge to lean my head on his shoulder, but fought it. It wasn't that I thought he would push me away—I was pretty sure he wouldn't. I just wasn't ready for where it may lead.

After the last video had played, I closed my laptop and looked at Mark. He blinked like he he'd woken from a trance, which comforted me a bit since I always felt a bit clouded when I stopped watching poetry videos.

"Those were really good. I can't believe people are that good at this stuff." He turned his body toward me just a bit more, so we were even more aligned.

My skinned warmed where he touched me. "I know. I love watching them because in a way it gives me this weird sort of confidence to write about whatever I want."

"What do you normally write about?" His eyes seemed to smolder. I was captivated by his words, by his lips as he spoke. Perhaps it wasn't the smartest move to watch poetry with him; it heightened my emotions, especially the romantic ones.

We were close enough that it would barely take any effort to close the distance. I was just thinking about leaning in, when my door opened with a ferocity that made us both jump back. We both wore guilty expressions. I had no desire to explain Mark to Dad.

But it wasn't Dad who stood in the doorway—it was Drea.

"Well, isn't this adorable. The nerd and the pariah. How incredibly touching." She mimed gagging and then laughed.

"What do you want, Drea?" I moved further away from Mark, my skin cool from the absence of his body heat.

"Just came up to see whose car is parked in the driveway. Your father pulled in right behind me, so I'm sure he wants to know too. Oh speaking of, hi, Walt," she called and gave a cheery wave.

Dad appeared in the doorway a moment later. His eyes scanned Mark and me, assessing the situation with a frown. He opened his mouth to speak, but then looked at Drea.

"Well, I've got homework," Drea said, and practically skipped from the doorway, no doubt delighted I was about to be lectured.

Dad focused his gaze on me. "Candace, what is going on here? And your face. I thought it was a minor accident?" The frown on his face shifted slightly to an expression of concern.

"I was just being clumsy," I said. "Mark came to bring me my assignments. We were working on English."

At the mention of Mark's name, my father once again narrowed his eyes.

"Hi, Mr. Ellis. It's nice to meet you." Mark stood to shake Dad's hand, and I saw a muscle in his jaw twitch when Dad shook it. Dad had probably applied extra pressure to the handshake.

"Thank you for bringing Candace her assignments," he said to Mark. Turning to me, he said, "Candace, we'll be having dinner soon. Your friend should get going." He left the room but was sure to push my door all the way open and turn to see if I'd gotten the message.

When he'd left, Mark came back to the desk and said, "I think he likes me."

“I’m so sorry. That was rude of him.” As if Drea barging in hadn’t been enough, Dad’s rudeness was over the line. I had a hard enough time keeping friends without Dad’s attitude.

“I can’t really blame him. If I found a devilishly handsome guy in my daughter’s room, I’d probably throw him out of the window.” He bent to collect his books.

“Devilishly handsome, huh?” I relaxed a little bit into my chair, hoping that my father hadn’t scared him off.

“Please don’t hurt my pride by telling me otherwise.” He smiled. “I should get moving.” He extended both of his hands to me and, without thinking, I took them. He pulled me from the chair with more force than I’d anticipated, and I wound up flush against his chest with my hands still in his.

My heart thudded in my chest. If I tilted my head just a little bit, our lips would meet. It took me a moment to talk myself out of it. Friends. That was what we were. I tried to stifle the sigh I felt when I backed up slightly, and Mark cleared his throat.

I led him downstairs and saw him out. “Try to stay out of trouble.” He smirked before I closed the door.

When I turned around to go back upstairs, Dad was standing a few feet away. His power stance prominent. “You know my rules about boys in your room. It hasn’t changed just because this is a new house.”

As much as I didn’t think he had a place to tell me about any rules, I wasn’t in the mood to argue. “I didn’t know he was coming over, and it felt like the only place to go that was mine. It won’t happen again.”

Dad stood there for a moment. He gaped at me; my response was not the one he expected.

“Is he your boyfriend?” Dad’s expression was one of deep discomfort, even his power stance faltered. Boys and dating had never been a strong talking topic for us.

“No, just a friend.” A friend whom I thought about kissing in my bedroom.

His expression cleared and looked more relaxed than before. “Good. You shouldn’t waste time on boys at your age.”

“I’ll keep that in mind.”

As I climbed the stairs, I thought about reminding him that he and Mom had been high school sweethearts, but it wasn’t the best example. When I got to my room, I took out my books to start the homework Mark had brought. It was hard to focus on metaphors when my mind kept wandering to Mark and how comfortable it was to sit with him, how he had looked at me with something like want.

I pulled out my phone and my fingers hovered over the screen. After a moment, I sent another apology to him. Was I looking for an excuse to talk to him? Maybe. My phone vibrated almost a minute later.

"Don't be. I had fun today."

"Me too," I typed.

"Maybe next time we should just skip school together. ;)"

He was probably kidding, but I couldn't think of a better way to spend a free day than with him.

CHAPTER 15

The days were getting colder and colder as we sped toward the end of fall. Light jackets were switched out for puffy ones and salt lines coated the boots most of us wore. Stores had already started selling salt for driveways. This winter was going to be a long one. My only comfort was that I wasn't going to have to spend it inside Dad's house.

Mark, Steve, and Greg were my new regular companions. When I wasn't at work, I was with them. They taught me about video games, and surprisingly I found that I enjoyed them. Mostly I liked just being a part of a group again. Even Steve had softened toward me. It helped that he beat me in almost every video game we played.

Outside of school, they were my crew, but I still ate lunch in the comfort of the almost-always-deserted library. The old, dusty books around me were all the company I needed—or so I told myself. I thought about venturing to the lunchroom again. Part of me was even hopeful that no one would throw anything my way, but I wasn't ready to be wrong. Humiliation was something I was used to, but still didn't go out of my way to experience.

The lunchroom was like a war zone. If I wasn't careful, I would step into enemy territory or I would hit a landmine. It would be easier to try if I had allies, but Mark hadn't made the slightest insinuation that I should join him. He joined me one or two days a week, but the days when he didn't, I felt lonelier than before he'd even started coming.

He had other friends, I knew that, but it was still hard to imagine him out there laughing with people. Enjoying the simple freedom of eating lunch with real people instead of those on book pages. It must have been, well, nice.

I was used to having free reign of the library during the lunch period. The librarian took advantage of the dead time to pull out her latest romance novel. I'd tried to covertly read the titles, but was often too far away. Not too far away, however, to often see shirtless men holding gasping women on the front covers.

I was reading a novel Mark had loaned me, a new one by James Patterson, when a shadow fell on the pages. I looked up, expecting to maybe see Mark with his lunch in hand, but was surprised at my redheaded visitor.

Shannon looked as unsure as I surely looked confused. I gaped at her foolishly, and it took a moment for me to realize that Shannon was waiting for me to move my bag from the only other chair at the table.

I scrambled quickly to move my things and gestured for her to sit. My mind raced with possibilities. When Mark and I had started hanging out, part of me had hoped it meant Shannon and I would somehow reconnect, and now, here she was.

She sat with her back straight. "So this is where you hide," Shannon said, examining the books spread around me.

"I didn't think my location was much of a mystery. Drea made sure everyone knew where I was in case they wanted to make my life miserable."

Shannon shook her head a bit. "I wouldn't know if she had. I'm not the one she tells things too—and even if I was, I would take everything she said with a pound of salt."

I pinched my wrist under the table, and was surprised when I felt pain. There was no scenario I could have imagined that involved Shannon seeking me out to have a conversation. Much less actually have a conversation where Drea was a topic.

"Most people just listen to her," I said.

"I'm aware. I know that firsthand," Shannon said, looking directly into my eyes. There was a steely glint that hadn't been there when we'd been friends, and I hated that I'd helped put it there.

Shannon played with the bracelet on her wrist while we sat there in awkward silence. I wondered how I could apologize to her for everything without making it seem like I was only doing it because I wasn't friends with Drea anymore. But truthfully, I didn't know if I ever *would* have apologized to her if I'd still been on team Drea.

I decided to cut to the chase. "What are you doing here, Shannon?"

Shannon almost looked grateful for my blunt question. "I'm here to tell you that you don't have to eat lunch in here if you don't want to. You can sit with us."

I couldn't help it—I laughed in her face. I felt bad the moment Shannon's expression hardened, but it really was just ridiculous.

"You don't believe me?" she asked, tone almost indignant.

"Don't take it personally. I just don't believe many people anymore."

"I couldn't imagine why." Her tone was dry.

I found Shannon's cool distance comforting. I could work with cool distance; it was seeing her broken that I couldn't handle.

"Look, I really don't care what you do. You can stay in here and hide until graduation if you'd like. I'm only here because Mark thinks it would be inappropriate for him to be the one to invite you, given our messy history. He's afraid of offending me somehow by bringing you around."

Humiliation filled me. "I'm sorry he asked you to do this," I said stiffly, trying to retain what was left of my pride.

"Don't be like that. Don't throw yourself a pity party."

"I'm not," I argued. "I just don't want other people to feel like they have to do things for me."

"Well, you don't know Mark that well. He does things for other people all the time. He's one of the good ones." Her voice softened when she talked about him. It made my stomach twist. It felt wrong to sit here and listen to Shannon talk about him like she knew him in ways I didn't. I knew that twisty feeling. It was unmistakably jealously, and I inwardly cursed myself for letting my feelings for Mark go unchecked.

"You like him," I accused.

Shannon jerked her head back and laughed. It was almost cruel. "You really did become shallow didn't you?"

Drea had slapped me, but that was nothing compared to the way Shannon was looking at me now. As if I meant nothing. As if my shallowness didn't surprise her.

"Whatever," Shannon said when I didn't respond. "For your information, not that I owe you any, I've got more important things on my mind than boys. I don't spend my day wondering who likes me or not."

Now that she'd said it, I remembered that even when we were younger, Shannon had never mentioned liking anyone: guy or girl.

"Sorry," I mumbled.

She nodded and I wasn't sure if that meant she forgave me or not, but her back relaxed and shoulders slouched a little.

She bit her lip as if she were debating whether or not to continue. "You should know Mark is a great guy, and he wants you around. That makes some of his friends, like me, nervous. And before you try to tell me you're just friends, save it. Steve already talked to me. You claiming to be his friend doesn't make me feel any better about it. You don't exactly have the best track record with friends either."

"I don't want to hurt him. I have no intention to," I said truthfully.

"I know, but you know what they say the road to hell is paved with." Shannon got up from her seat and pushed in her chair. She leaned on it slightly like the conversation had taken a lot out of her. "Listen, you can stay here like I said, but Mark wants you around, so think about it, okay?"

It wasn't the way I'd wanted my first real conversation with Shannon to go, but it had been civil, so I would take it. It wasn't until Shannon almost reached the exit that I called, "What important things do you have on your mind? Most girls our age really do put boys near the top of the priority list."

I meant it as a joke, but when Shannon turned, her face was serious. After a moment, when I was sure she was just going to walk out and not answer, she said quietly, "Getting the hell out of this town and never coming back."

Everything in me wanted to ask more, but she was already gone by the time I felt brave enough to.

***

I'd only felt this nervous one other time in my life, and it was at the beginning of senior year when I'd opened the same doors before me. Muffled noises of laughter and conversation filtered through the steel doors. I tried to convince myself that my fear of what lay beyond was absurd, but I felt my hands shake slightly as I pressed open the heavy doors.

The noise of my classmates laughing and talking was almost deafening. I was so used to the quiet of the library that this extreme noise made my ears ache. I moved slowly through the room, looking for Mark. I'd never paid attention to where anyone sat in the lunchroom. I'd only ever needed to sit next to Drea in the middle, where all eyes could be on us.

A few people shot me curious glances, but it wasn't nearly as bad as I thought it would be. As I scanned the crowd, I couldn't help but look in the direction of my old table. Drew was standing up behind Mindy, telling some story that made my old friends laugh.

Luke was the first to see me. For a moment, I thought he was going to wave me over, but then Drea put her hand on his arm to call him back to their discussion. When Luke didn't break eye contact with me, Drea followed his gaze. Her face registered confusion and then something very close to rage.

I wanted to turn around and go back to the safety my books, and I almost did, but then Mark called my name. I turned in the direction of his voice and he waved.

His table was at the far end of the lunchroom. Everyone at the table went silent when I walked up. A few of them looked at Shannon, who diffused a bit of the tension when she said, "Good to see you." Mark pointed to the empty seat between him and Shannon. It was the only empty seat at the table, and I took it.

"Hey, I'm glad you could make it," Mark said with just a bit too much excitement in his voice. He was clearly as nervous as I was, but trying to hide it.

"Me too." I smiled at him.

I looked down the table and saw Greg smiling at me, and Steve gave a slight nod when Greg elbowed him. Mark introduced me to the rest of the table. Some of them I'd seen before, but never spoken to. Most of them were halfway through eating, so they didn't give me their sole focus, which I was thankful for.

After a couple minutes of awkward introductions, the tension at the table—and in me—started to ease. Greg began telling an elaborate story about his refusal to dissect a frog that morning, effectively catching everyone's attention. He glanced quickly at me and gave me a sly wink. I needed to remember to thank him later.

"Is it everything you remember?" Mark asked. "Is it as gloriously mundane as you could have hoped?"

"It's more than I could have ever expected," I joked. I looked around at the students sitting at various tables, noting that nothing much had changed at all. Some of the faces weren't familiar to me, but the cliques were all the same. The way people confined themselves to specific tables based on their category of popularity seemed ridiculously childish to me now.

"In all seriousness, I'm happy you came. I've wanted to pull you out of there for a long time, but I didn't want to have it be awkward for you and Shannon."

"I get it and thanks. I shouldn't have even stayed there as long as I did."

We sat there eating lunch like it was just another day and for him it was, but for me, it felt like an accomplishment. It wasn't nearly as scary as I had thought it would be, and people didn't stare as much as I'd thought they would. A girl, Phoebe I thought her name was, even tried to include me in the debate about Pop Tarts or Toaster Strudels being the ultimate breakfast pastry. I wasn't sure who had started the conversation, but I would have put my money on Steve. He was more motivated by food than anyone I knew.

Luke looked over to me every few minutes. He swung his eyes away every time I caught him looking.

"If you're wondering if the conversation is always this enthralling, the answer is yes," Shannon drawled, which earned her a small glare from Steve. She merely shrugged, unaffected by his gaze.

"I'm glad I'm not the only one he glares at," I said lowly.

Shannon's lips turned up. "Believe me, it scares us more when he smiles instead of scowls."

"I wouldn't know. He hasn't exactly sent warm, fuzzy feelings my way."

Shannon turned a bit more toward me. A few people at our table sent her curious glances as she did so. "He takes a while to warm up. He barely spoke to me throughout our entire tenth grade year."

"I'd like to think that Greg and I soften him," Mark chirped.

"Sure you do," Shannon said, appeasing, but smiled at me when Mark turned toward Greg. "The only thing that softens Steve is food."

"Food. Got it."

"Candace," Rachel called from a table beside ours. Her friends' mouths were dropped open in wide "O's" as they watched her lean toward me. "Vinnie said you were the one who encouraged him to leave his number. We went out Saturday, so I guess I owe you a thank you."

Vinnie. The guy who always came into the theater and looked at Rachel like she walked on water. Someone had to step in and give them a push, so I'd decided last week that I was that person.

"It was just a matter of time," I said.

"I'm not so sure. We probably would have danced around each other forever," she said thoughtfully and turned back to her table with a final smile. Her friends bent their heads to whisper to her, but she shook them off.

I turned back to find Shannon watching me. When I raised my eyebrows at her, she raised hers back.

"I'm working on making peace with people."

"Yeah, Mark told me about the soda incident and your apology to her. How's it feel?"

"How does what feel?"

"To make amends."

It took me a moment to find the right words. "It feels…satisfying somehow."

"I'm sure. Apologies can go a long way for both parties," she said.

The weight of her words wasn't lost on me. I'd never apologized to her, and now wasn't the right time. We were too surrounded. Still, there was something else I wanted to tell her. As I was about to speak, I caught a steely glare from the other side of the room.

Drea and I faced each other. A shiver of unease ran through me, not just for me but for Mark and the other people around me too.

As Mark pulled me into conversation, I tried to push down the feeling that I was wearing a bull's eye. But even if Drea was planning something, how bad could it be? What more could they possibly do to me? Looking at Mark, Shannon, Greg, and even Steve, I realized the stakes were higher now. I had more to lose than before.

Chapter 16

As I sat in my car, I wanted to believe the past week had been filled with the right moves. The week had been calm, pleasant even. Coming out of hiding, helping Rachel, talking to Shannon, all of that had to mean things were looking up. I didn't hate my life anymore, and with the year I'd had, that was an accomplishment.

I was scribbling down the last bit of English homework when I heard the familiar tap on my window. Mark's knuckles wrapping on my window had become a new sort of reminder bell—I wasn't even startled by him anymore.

It was warm today for late November, and Mark had foregone the jacket and opted for jeans and a t-shirt. I didn't think it was warm enough for short sleeves, but I didn't hate the way his biceps looked in them either. Mark greeted me with a smile; the one that always made me feel a bit warm.

I didn't exactly wait in my car for him every morning. It just so happened that I'd taken to sitting in my car to finish homework I could have easily completed the night before, and Mark happened to come get me every morning.

Slinging my backpack over my shoulder, I walked beside him toward school. He walked close to me. People had stopped staring at our proximity a day or two before. They'd been interested in us at first. I was the girl who'd broken Luke's heart, and it was like a sin for me to move on.

"Was that English you were finishing up?" Mark asked. From his slightly annoyed tone, I knew it wasn't the first time he'd asked the question.

"It was," I said, feeling guilty for spacing out.

"Slacker." It had quickly become his favorite thing to call me. Probably because he knew I was the exact opposite.

"I just like to take my time on my work. You can't rush perfection, you know."

"I see. And here I thought you were waiting for me."

"Keep dreaming," I said and nudged him with my shoulder.

We headed for Mark's locker as we did every morning before chemistry.

Looking back, it was probably the routine of our morning walk and the lack of chatter from Drea all week that gave us both, especially me, the sense of safety. Perhaps, had Drea acted earlier in the week, I would have been more on guard.

As Mark pulled open his locker door, there was a loud *POP* and reddish brown liquid projected from it. I closed my eyes against the oncoming assault and brought my hands up too late, as I felt cool globs land on my face and hair.

Peeking out from under my lashes, I realized none of the goo had landed in my eyes. When I saw the condition of Mark and his locker, I wished I kept my eyes closed longer.

He looked like he'd just finished with a live sacrifice. His body and face were covered. There was no mirror in his locker, not that I really cared to see my reflection, but I had a feeling I didn't look much better.

Mark stood paralyzed with what I thought was shock, but after a moment, I realized it was something else entirely. The only part of him that moved was his Adam's apple. I hadn't known him long enough to understand his body language as an expert would, but I knew rage when I saw it.

"I'm so sorry," I whispered and heard my voice crack. I had made him a target. I had done this to him.

Mark's body tightened, but still he didn't move. "Why would you—"

"You guys look like those losers from that movie," Mindy said. "You know, the one where the weird girl goes psycho at prom." Her red lips were spread wide, loving the havoc in front of her.

Some people stopped to stare, some looked sympathetic, but Drea and company, Luke included, looked victorious.

This was Luke's handiwork. Drea had been the brains, but Luke had been the one to rig the locker. I'd seen Luke and Drew do it once before to a boy who'd flirted with me last year. As I looked at Luke now, I didn't know how to reconcile the boy who had been sweet to me, who I'd given everything to, with the one standing before me now. But the cruel streak had always been there. I saw that now. How had I been so blind?

I moved forward to… what? Fight Drea? Snap at Luke?

I felt strong hands touch my waist. Mark didn't force me to stop my approach, but his touch, which was so unexpected, made me falter. I paused only for a moment and then allowed him to pull me back to his chest. I could feel the race of his heartbeat beneath his shirt. Even covered in some unnamable substance, his presence calmed me.

"You do know how that movie ends, don't you?" Mark asked. The sharpness of his voice reminded me of how winter wind could cut through anything. It was the first time I'd heard him sound like that.

"Is that a threat?" Luke stepped forward, stretching out his arms. He'd never looked stupid to me until that moment. We'd laughed at jocks in movies, and he'd said, "Those meatheads give us all a bad name." Now, walking forward cracking his knuckles, he looked like every teensploitation movie cliché we'd ever made fun of.

"Nope. Just pointing out how stupid the reference was in this situation." He adopted a casual pose. Luke didn't intimidate him, and it showed.

"Are you calling us stupid?" Luke half shouted. His hands were clenched like he couldn't wait for his fist to connect with Mark's face. His eyes moved back and forth from where Mark held my waist and Mark's face. I wasn't sure, but I swore Mark's grip tightened every time Luke's eyes landed on his hands.

"If he doesn't, I will," Greg said as he and Steve came to stand beside Mark. I hadn't seen them approach, but their presence was more than welcome.

"Need your boyfriends to help you?" Luke spat. "I'd keep an eyes on your friends. She's got a history."

My stomach twisted, heat flooding my veins.

Mark lunged forward. "What did you just say?"

Just then, the morning bell sounded. Some students around us started to move, but most stayed rooted to the spot, afraid to miss the show.

Drea stood between Mark and Luke and whispered something in Luke's ear that sounded a lot like "later," but I couldn't be sure.

"It's not worth it," I told Mark. He stayed put at first, ready for a fight. But after a few tugs from Drea, Luke turned and stalked down the hallway, shaking Drea off as he did so. She was left to catch up to him, and Mindy and Allison were left to catch up to her.

Mark looked into his locker and picked up a couple of his books to shake them off. It was clear that it was a wasted effort; nothing in there was salvageable.

I had to find a way to pay for everything ruined.

"You two okay?" Steve asked. His tone had malice in it. I'd heard him be curt, even borderline mean, but never murderous.

"I'm okay," I said as Mark nodded.

"I'm heading home. Care to join me?" His body still carried a bit of the residual tension from the confrontation, but his voice didn't.

"You're just leaving?" Greg asked before I could answer.

Mark turned to him and spread out his arms. "I'm definitely not going to walk around all day in this. I have no idea what it is, but it feels gross, and I'm trying to breathe through my mouth in case the smell makes me gag."

The globs that covered my face and hair hadn't dried, but it would be especially unpleasant if I didn't shower before they did.

"Point taken. Let us know if you need anything," Greg said before he and Steve made their way to first period. Steve nudged my shoulder as he walked away. "You too, okay?"

I could only nod as he walked away. His kindness was as unexpected as the lump forming in my throat.

Mark looked at me and repeated, "Care to join me?"

I looked down at my jeans and sweater. "Yeah, I'll call my dad to tell him I got sick before attendance in first period."

Mark didn't bother to shut his locker before we walked down the almost deserted hallway quietly. We drew stares from a few stragglers, but by some miracle, we made it out of the school without being spotted by a teacher. They would most certainly have questions when they saw the condition of Mark's locker, and some answer, not the truth of course, would have to be given. The truth would lead to more torture from Drea and her minions.

We took one car to Mark's house. Mark insisted on taking his car despite my protests.

"I can't let you ruin the interior of that car," Mark persisted until I relented and got in.

I felt terrible every time I caught sight of the reddish brown stains on the interior. Even though it wasn't as new as the car I drove, I still didn't feel right staining it.

"My dad's at work for the day," Mark informed me as we pulled into the driveway of his Cape Cod style home. It looked cozy on the outside, so different from Dad's.

I wasn't surprised that the entryway of his home was filled with books, but what did surprise me was that Mark and Vincent were able to go in and out of the house without knocking them over every morning. I envisioned the stacks falling like dominos.

"Sorry for the tight quarters," Mark said sheepishly. "These are the books Dad hasn't catalogued yet."

"Why doesn't he get them sent to the store?" I asked, looking at a couple of the titles.

Mark held up his hands. "I've asked him to hundreds of times, but he wants to inspect them before they're brought into the store or something."

That logic didn't quite make sense to me, but I liked that Vincent was passionate enough about his work to take it home with him. I hoped I found something I loved that much one day.

We made our way to the kitchen where we put our bags down on the island counter. My mother would've been impressed with how clean each surface was. The sparkle and shine may have rivaled her kitchen.

"Want anything to drink?" Mark asked. He opened a cupboard and grabbed a glass.

"I think I'm good for right now." My hands were mostly free of gunk, but I still didn't want to dirty anything else.

"There are two bathrooms. If you want to shower, you're welcome to," he said, reading my mind.

I touched one finger to my hair and felt the crispy pieces. It reminded me of my hair-gelling faze in eighth grade. I'd looked like a poodle. Every time I looked at pictures from those years, I wondered what had convinced me it looked attractive. It had taken me years to convince mom to take them off the walls.

"That would be amazing," I said.

Mark led me to one of the bathrooms on the second floor. It took him only a minute to get a towel and excuse himself.

I turned on the shower and adjusted it until steam started to rise from the raining water. Undressing and leaving my clothes in a pile on the floor, I stepped into the warmth. The water ran over my body and eased the tension out of my knotted muscles.

The only soap in the bathroom smelled fresh and distinctly like Mark. I gently scrubbed my face and arms first. The caked on substance was easier to remove than I thought it would be. The mess in my hair, however, was not. I worked shampoo through with my fingers carefully, like trying to untie the world's most delicately tangled twine.

A slight knock on the door made me jump. Mark's muffled voice was barely audible from the other side.

"Come in," I called. I almost brought my hands to shield myself, but realized how ridiculous that was. Mark couldn't see through the dark shower curtain without Superman vision. Thinking of the messy pile I'd left my clothes in, I wished I had tucked my delicates into my other clothing.

"I brought you some of my clothes. Just sweatpants and a shirt. I'll throw your clothes in the washer if you want, so you can wear them home later." He sounded a bit unsure.

"That would be great, thank you." Now I definitely wished I had folded my clothes. Hopefully Mark wouldn't picture me in the worn cotton undies I decided to wear today. Not that I wanted him to picture me in any underwear.

Sticking my head out from behind the shower curtain, I saw that I was alone again. Mark had gone out silently.

I decided to forego a second round of shampooing and turned off the water. The moment I pulled the curtain back, goosebumps rose on my skin. The events of the day set in and I couldn't help shivering as I toweled the droplets of water off.

I wrapped my hair in the towel and quickly put on the clothes Mark had set out. I welcomed the warmth they provided. The clothes were far too big, but they were comfortable. When I examined my reflection in the mirror, I thought of the times I'd tried on Austin's clothes. As a child I'd often wandered into his closet. I'd loved the way his clothing swallowed me. One time when he came in the room and found me, he'd laughed and put his ball cap on my head. He called me "little bro" from then on out. Even when he went into high school and we didn't talk as much, we still had that joke.

When I came out of the bathroom, Mark was nowhere in sight. Curiosity guided me down the hallway. It only took me two tries to find his room. It was just as I thought it would be: clean and organized. My own room currently had enough clothing on the floor to cover the majority of the carpet, but his were all put away neatly.

"Snooping?" Mark asked. He leaned against the doorway with his arms crossed, but his posture was relaxed. His hair was wet and the stains on his face were gone. He'd traded his stained clothing for basketball shorts and a plain white t-shirt. The shirt hugged him in a way that made my stomach clench.

"Observing," I quipped.

"Well, don't let me stop you." He waved his hand forward, giving me free reign.

There wasn't much to snoop through. Mark's room was pretty sparse. I sat on his bed, which was cornered to the far wall, and observed that he had nothing on his walls, any photos or posters, not even a calendar. "Not a fan of decorations?"

Mark came to sit on the open space beside me. He was close, but not close enough that our bodies touched. "I've never liked anything enough to want to look at it every time I come in here."

"You don't like certain people enough to hang their photos?"

"There's one photo, but I keep that in here." He shifted his body slightly and reached for his wallet on his bedside table. When he flipped it open, a picture of a beautiful woman was prominently displayed. Gently, I took the wallet out of his hands and examined the picture. There was no doubt about who the woman was. She had the same broad smile as her son.

"I like to keep her with me, not just tacked up on the wall," Mark said as I handed the wallet back to him.

"That makes sense. She's beautiful," I said softly.

"She was." Mark returned the wallet and cleared his throat. "How are you after this morning?"

"I'm fine. I should be asking you how you are."

"It was just my books and clothes, no big deal."

It was a big deal to me. He had been targeted because of me, his kindness in not laying blame at my feet was more than I deserved.

"I'm sorry," I whispered, trying to choke down the stone in my throat. I turned my face away, unable to look at him.

"For what?"

"Everything. They only did that stuff to you because they hate me."

"Hey, you don't know that. I'm hateable." He knocked my shoulder with his own, clearly trying to lighten my mood.

"No, you're not." Our shoulders still touched and neither of us shifted to separate. I lifted my head to see him and found him looking down at me.

"They're the worst kind of people." He brought his hand hesitantly to my cheek and wiped away a tear. His hand lingered there for a moment before bringing it back to his lap.

"I was one of them." My cheek felt hot where his fingers had traced my skin.

"Not anymore," he said softly.

My brain wasn't working correctly. For once, it seemed to agree with my fast-beating heart.

I lifted my head and parted my lips just before they met his. The electricity from our lips travelled throughout my body, sending tiny sparks to every limb. Mark's body tensed as his mouth moved against mine.

When I pulled back slightly, his eyes smoldered down at me, searching for something I couldn't name.

"I don't want you to kiss me because you're upset." His voice was low and gravelly.

"That's not why I did it," I breathed, wanting only to keep on kissing him.

He stared at me for a moment longer, as if assessing the truth in my words. "I don't want you to take this back," he said thickly.

"I won't."

Slowly, like he was afraid I would change my mind, he brought his hand gently to my face and cupped my cheek as he bent his head to mine. Once our lips met, every ounce of him that had been restrained before seemed to break free, and he kissed me like I was what he needed to survive. Like his heart would cease to beat if he released me. I crushed myself against him, trying to bring our bodies as close as possible. Electricity shot through me in frustrating and euphoric ways it never had before, and all I knew was that I needed more of it.

I didn't know how long we stayed in each other's arms, but when we finally separated I was the perfect kind of breathless.

CHAPTER 17

Our hands were laced. We were in full view of anyone who looked at us as we passed. I wasn't sure when we'd decided to test the waters of a romantic relationship, but there was nowhere to go but forward after our kiss. Well, kisses really. There'd been a lot of them the previous night, and by the time Mark had driven me back to my car, my lips were red and raw. More than just the kissing, I loved the feeling of my hand in his. It had been me, after all, who had reached for his this morning.

People could have been looking, they probably were, but I didn't care. Other eyes didn't matter when his were on me, looking at me with the same desire he had when he'd kissing me the night before.

We bypassed our lockers and headed straight toward chem. Neither of us wanted to know if there were more surprises in store just yet.

"All right, let's keep moving on the notes from yesterday," Mr. Mason called after the bell. He turned and began marking up the whiteboard at the front of the classroom.

I was relieved that we weren't doing any new labs—I was sure I would drop any beaker I touched. I felt jittery next to Mark. We'd been partners for a while, but now I was aware of how closely we sat, how his arm sometimes brushed mine when he scribbled notes. Concentrating took more effort than it usually did, and I momentarily wondered if he was as aware of my presence as I was of his. I looked at him. He looked fully engaged in Mr. Mason's lecture, but after a moment a smile spread across his lips. His leg brushed against me, causing me to jump, and his smile widened.

"You should really pay attention," he whispered.

"You're not making it easy."

At the end of the period, Shannon came over. "Looks like Greg won the bet," she said, looking put out.

"Bet?" Mark and I said together.

"Don't be mad, but we all had a slight wager on when you two would give up the 'just friends' line. Greg's guess was the closest to today. Had you held out another week, I would be roughly two-hundred dollars richer."

"Are we transparent enough that you guys placed bets?" Mark asked. He was smiling, taking his friends' actions in stride.

"Well, you definitely are," Shannon said, nodding toward Mark, "but Candace was the wild card. I was sure she would hold out longer."

"Thanks for the vote of confidence," I said. I wasn't quite sure what to make of the bet, but Shannon didn't make it seem like their friends were against our relationship.

"Anytime. Steve is going to be pissed. His guess was one day after Greg's."

"Well, I'm sure he'll be in a lovely mood when we see him then," I grumbled.

"Eh. Buy him a cookie at lunch. He'll get over it," Shannon suggested.

"Better make it a slice of pizza. We'll need the big guns for this one," Mark said.

***

In the following weeks, Mark and I fell into an easy routine, like we'd been dating for longer than we actually had. It worried Mom a bit that I spent the majority of my time with him, but I knew she would like him when she met him.

We usually worked the same shifts at the movie theater, although I was pretty sure I'd seen him switch shifts with Rachel on more than one occasion. I had to admit it was nice that we frequently worked together. If we didn't, we wouldn't have been able to spend nearly as much time together as Robbie had put me back on the schedule for almost every Friday and Saturday night.

For his part, Joe loved working with us. He took any chance he could to remind us that our relationship was really a credit to his matchmaking skills; he seized on opportunities to launch into much more dramatic retellings of our first few shifts together. "Anyone of less romantic prowess," he said, "would have thought the tension between the two was hatred, but I knew they were just itching to rip each other's clothes off."

A steady balance seemed to have been struck at home as well. Drea was civil to May, although she snuck in jabs about the new baby whenever the opportunity presented itself. She ignored me, which I put in the win column. I was afraid that, after the locker incident, home would be a battleground, but it was all quiet on the Drea front.

Thanksgiving passed without incident, and I put on false smiles at the dinner table. Dad seemed pleased with my effort there, and that was good because I'd sent my Dartmouth application out just before the long weekend. Dad hadn't tried to force the baby conversation again. I thought he was going for the laidback approach, waiting for me to be ready to accept him and his family-to-be. He would be waiting a long time.

Mark had asked about Dad a couple times, but stopped when he saw how much it hurt. In some ways, it was harder for me to talk about how I felt for Dad than how much I missed Austin.

The diner had become a part of our routine, and even though we ordered the same thing, sat in the same booth, it never felt monotonous. When we were together, nothing felt like going through the motions. Sometimes Greg and Steve joined us, but today we were alone and able to be the couple others rolled their eyes at. The ones who held hands across the table and giggled when the other said something only moderately funny.

Carly frequently shot us "I told you so" looks, but I couldn't have cared less.

"I think we should see a movie tomorrow," Mark said around bites of pancakes.

"I can't. I've got that history exam Monday. Studying has got to happen tomorrow, since it's not happening tonight." A dollop of syrup lay on his lower lip, and I was momentarily distracted by how his lips would taste.

"This is what I get for dating a smart girl. Focused, determined, and can't be swayed." His tongue licked his lip slowly, and there was a mischievous twinkle in his eye.

"Please, I recall you staying in all day until your shift last Saturday because you had a test on Monday." I pushed my plate of food away from me.

"I don't see what's so bad about that."

"You had Sunday off. You could have studied that day."

Mark started shaking his head. "I don't believe in cramming the day before."

"Well, you have your way, and I have mine."

"I love your independence," he laughed, and I nudged his leg under the table. "What? It's a turn on."

Loud smacking on the window caused us both to jump a bit. The forecast had said freezing rain was possible, but the sky had looked okay when we'd pulled in the parking lot.

"Shit. I left the sunroof cracked. I'll be right back." He sprung up from the booth and took off quickly.

I wasn't sure what good closing the sunroof would be now. There was no way his cloth interior wasn't wet. He was the only person I knew who liked the sunroof cracked in December.

I watched him run out of the restaurant, passing Luke as he did so. Luke only glanced at him briefly before making his way toward his family. He spotted me and I met his eyes before turning to focus on my phone.

Luke was with his family every Saturday when Mark and I came in for breakfast. Luke's mother always called out a hello, but had stopped inviting me over when she realized Mark and I were a couple.

Someone approached. Looking up, I saw Luke only a few feet away. My back tensed, bracing for whatever was coming. He had been careful to avoid me after what had happened with Mark's locker, but it appeared avoidance was over.

Without waiting to be invited to sit, he slid into the seat across from me. "Hey. I saw your date run out. Trouble in paradise?" He smiled. Everything about him appeared casual and friendly, but I knew him.

As he sat in front of me, I detected something familiar. I'd seen it before when I'd made polite conversation with guys at parties while I'd waited for him to get done with whatever drinking game was popular that weekend. Jealousy. It was clear as day in the way his eyes narrowed and eyebrows creased. It sharpened his features.

"He had to get something out of his car," I said, defensively.

"And left you all alone for someone to swoop in." He smirked. He'd always been overly confident. Why had I found that attractive?

"What do you want, Luke?"

His smirk faltered at my harsh tone. “I’ve been thinking a lot lately. Seeing you around with Mike—”

“Mark,” I interjected.

“Whatever. It’s just seeing you with him has got me thinking—”

“Hey bud, I think you’re in my seat.” Mark stood only a foot or two behind me. Luke’s presence had distracted me enough that I hadn’t even realized he’d come back in the diner. His jacket was discolored from the rain, and his cheeks were red, but I suspected not from the weather outside.

“What if I don’t feel like moving?” Luke purred, trying to get a rise out of Mark.

Mark put his hands on the back of my seat and gripped tightly. “Then I could assist you.” He kept his voice low, so other tables wouldn’t hear the confrontation.

Sending a smug look in Mark’s direction, Luke crossed his arms and stayed seated. For a moment, I wasn’t sure how everything would play out. Watching Luke and Mark stare each other down reminded me of dogs fighting over a bone. It irritated me that I was the bone in the scenario.

Luke finally barked a laughed and inched out of the seat. “Just messing with you,” he said and slapped Mark on the shoulder with more force than necessary.

Mark shot daggers at Luke as he called Carly for the bill. Annoyance filtered through me, and I found it difficult to not snap at Mark when he tried to talk to me. He elected to stay quiet while we paid the bill.

The tension between us didn’t ease as Mark drove me back to Dad’s house. There was a chill between us that had never been there before. When Mark pulled the car into the driveway and shut off the engine, he turned to me with an apologetic face.

“I’m not sure why you’re mad, but you haven’t uncrossed your arms since I interrupted your conversation with Luke.” Mark’s tone turned sour at the mention of Luke’s name.

“This has nothing to do with Luke,” I said and rolled my eyes.

“No? It kinda seems like it does.”

“I’m not a chew toy,” I burst out.

Mark looked at me in confusion. No doubt replaying what, exactly, had taken place at the diner. "I'm not following you."

"I don't want to be something you and Luke have a pissing match over. You have no idea how low that makes me feel. Some girls love guys getting worked up over them, but I don't. I'm not property. Understand?"

Luke had acted like I was his countless times, and I'd loved it. But distance had brought me clarity. I hated that I'd been so willing to let him own me. So much so that when he had left me, I was lost. I was not going to let that happen with Mark.

Mark was silent for a moment, like he was mulling over everything I'd said. Finally, he sank back into his seat. "He gets to me, not that it's an excuse. You're not, what did you say, a chew toy? I know that." He tentatively reached out to take my hand and relief flooded his features when I let him. "I really am sorry."

I let out a calming breath. Leaning over, I planted a light kiss on his lips. "I let him own me," I said quietly. "I let him dictate everything, and I won't do that again. I really like you, but I won't let anyone own me again."

"I don't want to own you. I just want to be a part of your world. I'm sorry," he said again.

"You're my boyfriend. Not Luke. Just remember that," I said and ran my fingers through his hair.

"I know. It's not easy knowing he was your boyfriend before me, but I need to get over it."

"Jealous?" I said, arching my eyebrows.

"Unfortunately and humiliatingly, yes." He leaned his forehead against mine.

I took his face in my hands and looked directly into his eyes. "This is new. We get a bit of a learning curve."

"That's probably a good thing." He leaned in to kiss me and just when I thought he was going to pull back, he wrapped his arms around me and brought me closer. It wasn't easy to maneuver in his sedan, but somehow I managed to make it to his side of the car with my chest against his. It was only when I remembered that we were in full view of the house's front window that I pulled back, making Mark groan in frustration. It took me several seconds to convince myself to go in and get ready for work instead of kissing him again.

Chapter 18

Notes and cue cards for my history test were fanned out in front of me. I'd been studying all day. It wasn't the ideal way to spend my Sunday, but it was the last big test before midterms.

I was looking over notes on the Gettysburg Address when I heard knocking on my window. Luke.

Approaching the window, I noticed how disheveled he looked and how glassy his eyes were. He'd been drinking…but it wasn't my job to worry about him anymore.

"Drea's not here. She's still at her dad's," I called through the glass.

"I'm not here for Drea. Let me in." He tapped his knuckles against the glass.

"No. Go home, Luke." I went to pull the shade, but as I got closer, I noticed his eyes weren't glassy. They were wet. I paused with my hand on the shade.

"I just want to talk. Please," his voice broke.

I knew would probably regret it later, but I flipped the latch and opened the window. I walked the center of the room to put enough space between us. "Say what you have to say and then go. I've got studying to do."

He stepped closer, so he was within only a couple feet of me. "Don't be like that. I just want to finish our conversation from yesterday."

I shook my head in disgust. "You've been an asshole to me for months and you want me to be nice to you?" My temper flared.

"I know that I've been a dick, but I've really been thinking these past few weeks, really before that. I just didn't know how to tell you, but then I saw you with *him*, and it clicked."

I didn't like where this was going. It felt wrong to be having a conversation like this in my bedroom. Especially after my argument with Mark yesterday.

Raising my hand to stop him, I said, "I really don't think I want to hear it, and I don't think Drea would either."

At the mention of her name, his lip curled. "Drea? That was a mistake and you know it. She's a nightmare. I only hooked up with her because…I needed to get back at you."

"It doesn't matter why you hooked up with her. The point is that you did, and you moved on," I tried to reason with him. "Like me."

"Does this look like moving on?" He splayed his arms out as if he wanted me to take a good look at him. "I haven't moved on. Anytime I try, I end up missing you more. I miss how it was. It was easy between us, wasn't it?"

I opened my mouth to ask if he had been in a different relationship than I, but when I really thought about it, things had been easy. Not because we'd gotten along so well; it was easy because I'd gone out of my way to put his needs before my own.

"At times it was," I conceded and when he reached for me, I stepped back and added, "but I think you're just remembering all the good parts. We weren't a perfect match, Luke."

"You're only saying that because of him," he sneered, veins in his neck bulging.

"No, I'm saying that because time showed me we weren't. Your actions after you broke up with me showed me that we weren't. How I feel now shows me weren't."

"You cheated. How did you expect me to react?" He grabbed some of the hair sticking out of his ball cap.

Frustration filled me. "I'm not going through this again. You wouldn't be here if you thought I cheated. You're here because you realized you fucked up when you trusted Drea. You've been sleeping with the devil. How's that feel?" The hurtful words spewed from my lips like I was breathing fire. I didn't want to hurt him exactly, but I needed this, whatever it was, to finally end. If my words hurt, so be it.

I expected him to fire back, but he didn't. He hung his head in what could only be shame. "I can't believe we got to this place," he whispered. When he looked at me, I saw how wet his face was.

"I know," I softened. How many times had I thought that exact thing?

"We can go back. It can all go back to the way it was. There has to be parts of it that you miss." He pulled me to him before I could react, buried his hands in my hair, and lowered his mouth to mine.

It was the moment I'd been wishing for since he'd left me. He was offering me my old life back. All I had to do was kiss him back, and we would go back to how we had been. The fantasy had run through my head hundreds of times, and in every one, I always went back to Luke. It was almost surreal to push him away.

"I don't want to go back." I didn't know when I had started crying, but the taste of salt surprised me.

"I don't believe you." He moved like might grab me again. I braced myself, but he stopped just before he touched me. "You wanted this all back before your new boyfriend. You wanted *me* back. You think I didn't see the way you looked at me before him?"

Luke waved off whatever answer I was going to give him and stalked toward the window. He was halfway out when I reached him.

Grabbing his arm, I held it until he looked at me. "Mark has nothing to do with my decision," I said and kept his gaze, willing him to see reason.

For a moment, I thought maybe I had broken through.

"Bullshit," Luke said and yanked his arm free.

Once his body cleared the window, I slammed it shut and pulled the shade, shaking. There was something broken in Luke, and it would make him do something stupid one day. I just knew it.

Going back to my bed, I tried to concentrate on my notes, but my mind kept wandering to Luke and how his focus had been on Mark.

CHAPTER 19

The cold air pierced through my jacket as I looked over my notecards. The wind made them flutter in my hand. The day was gray all around, like somehow nature knew what was about to happen.

Mark was already ten minutes later than he usually was, and anxiety flooded me with each passing minute. Luke had left angry last night, but he wasn't mean enough to do anything dangerous—or so I hoped.

I pulled out my phone to call Mark again, but as I did, a text came in.

"Flat tire. Be in later."

He followed it with a picture. One flat tire was really two, and they looked like they had some help getting flat. Slashes were visible even in the grainy photo.

Stuffing my phone back into my pocket without responding, I marched toward the school, determined to end this. They could do whatever to me, but Mark was off limits.

Luke was nowhere to be found. It was like he knew I'd come looking for him. If I couldn't get to him, I would get to her. Drea had helped Luke somehow. I knew it. I knew *them*.

A quick glance at my watch told me exactly where she would be. With five minutes left before the bell, Drea and crew would be in the bathroom applying last-minute makeup touches to cover all the imperfections and devil horns underneath.

I flung the door to the bathroom open with such force that Allison, the door guard, went stumbling forward.

"What the fuck?" she yelled, clutching her back where the door had struck her. It was the first time in four years I'd heard her voice go above the level of a whisper.

Mindy went to Allison's side and rubbed her back, as if slow circles and glaring at me could take the pain away.

"Lost?" Drea spat. She didn't turn to help Allison. Instead, she continued to apply another layer of nude lipstick.

"What the hell is wrong with you?" I seethed.

Drea capped the lipstick and turned around. "You mean other than your presence?"

"You can hate me all you want, but you don't get to fuck with Mark. Slashing his tires, really?"

Her eyes widened a fraction. It lasted only a second before her cool demeanor was in place once more. Drea had done a lot of terrible things to a lot of people, but the surprise on her face was a giveaway. She knew nothing about Mark's car.

But knowing that did nothing to abate my anger. I may not have had Luke in front of me, but Drea was a suitable target. She was guilty of a lot, even if it wasn't what I'd come to berate her for.

"You didn't know! That's rich. What happened, Drea? Miss the part where Luke realized you weren't shit anymore?"

"Shut your mouth," Drea warned.

"Why? Embarrassed for your entourage to hear just how little you mean to the guy you destroyed me to have? He didn't even introduce you to his mother!" I was loud enough that anyone outside the door could hear.

Mindy and Allison looked at Drea in clear confusion. It was clear she had told them something very different about her relationship with Luke.

Drea's chest heaved up and down, and Mindy and Allison moved to get behind me. I cursed myself for letting my emotions get the better of me. Three on one wasn't going to be pretty, and I was sure I was going to walk out with more than a split lip. We all stood tensed. Ready. Waiting.

At the opening of the door, we turned to see who the intruder was.

"Well, I feel like I've interrupted something," Shannon said, her expression calm.

In the presence of someone outside of the situation, Drea composed herself. She turned to the mirror and brushed her hands through her hair nonchalantly.

Allison and Mindy knew the cue to follow her, so they, too, took last looks in the mirror. Without acknowledging Shannon, Drea led them out, but stopped when she was shoulder to shoulder with me. "You should have stayed hidden. Anything that happens now is on you."

When the door closed behind them, I felt my body wilt. I grabbed the sink to steady myself. It felt cool under my shaking hands. I didn't even have to look in the mirror to know that my face was burning red.

"Good morning?" Shannon said sarcastically.

"Just the average one in this high school." I tried to smile, but my mouth barely twitched. "Lucky you came in when you did."

"I would love to tell you that I just happened to stroll in, but I saw you tear down the hallway and fly in here. When you didn't come out, I figured I better come make sure they weren't drowning you in the toilet or something."

We both laughed.

"In all seriousness, thank you for looking out for me."

She nodded and rested her hip against the sink. "Full disclosure, Mark texted me and asked me to. Apparently, he was concerned after you didn't text him back."

At the mention of Mark, my heart sank. Even when he wasn't physically here, he looked out for me, and all he would get was more slashed tires and torment for his troubles.

"They won't stop doing this to him, and I just made it worse. I wasn't thinking when I came in here…I fucked up."

"Hey, it's okay," she said and put her hand on my forearm. "There's only so much one person can take." For the first time since middle school, Shannon looked at me like we were friends. Like she sympathized with my pain and commended my effort.

The bell sounded, jarring us out of whatever moment we were in the middle of. I splashed water on my face to try and take some of the redness out of it.

When we emerged from the bathroom, the hallway was almost empty. There were just a few tardy students hustling toward the classrooms. Down the hall, Drea had Luke cornered with a murderous look. After everything the night before, I was beginning to think maybe the two of them really deserved each other.

Mark's chair sat empty throughout chemistry. It took all I had to focus on my history exam and not check my phone to see if he had texted, which it turned out he hadn't. His silence frustrated me almost as much as his absence did.

Mark hadn't been absent once since we'd gotten together. Without him here, I wasn't sure if I had a place. I sat with *his* friends at lunch. I spoke to *his* friends in the hallways.

I decided to head to the library for lunch like I had before, but Shannon was waiting at the entrance.

When I came to a halt in front of her, she said, "I thought you'd wind up here."

"I was just…I didn't know if…I was just returning a book."

"Really?"

I held up a book I wasn't actually done reading as if it were proof.

"Good. Return it and then let's go."

I stood still for a moment until she raised her eyebrows at me. It took me only a moment to put the book in the return slot. I was going to have to come back for that later.

"You don't have to do this," I said as we made our way to the cafeteria.

"Do what?"

"Babysit me because Mark isn't here."

She stopped short before the doors to cafe. "I'm not babysitting you."

"No?"

"No. I'm helping someone who used to be…who maybe is my friend." There was an awkwardness to her voice and a hardness that I didn't understand.

Shannon's ability to never stop surprising me was unmatched. Friend was a word I never expected her to use around me again.

Shannon pushed open the doors in front of her. "Are you coming?"

***

Mark was waiting in my driveway when I arrived home. The car he was leaned up against was newer than the one he normally drove, and I recognized it to be Vincent's. I'd seen it enough times in the parking lot of the bookstore to recognize it.

I'd had time to think about everything today. I was responsible for his car. I might not have actually vandalized it, but he hadn't even been on their radar until he started dating me. I couldn't let him be my punching bag.

His arms were around me the moment I got out of the car. Somehow he seemed to know that I needed some sort of reassurance, but I felt immensely guilty that he was comforting me and not the other way around.

"It's okay," he whispered and kissed my hair.

"No, it's really not. This is my fault."

"Really, did you slash my tires?" he asked, laughing.

I pulled away from him suddenly, not amused. How could he possibly think what happened today was funny? I'd spent the better half of the day mustering up the courage to give Mark the option of leaving me. It would crush me if he chose to walk away, but I couldn't expect him to hang on if he would always have to look over his shoulder. I'd lived like that for months; I would never ask anyone else to.

"What's going on in that head of yours?" he asked, touching my temple lightly.

"I just think maybe we should talk," I said.

He grimaced. "I don't have a lot of experience with girls, but when the words 'we need to talk' are said, it usually doesn't end well." He tried to keep his tone light, but when I finally looked at him, his eyes held the seriousness of someone about to lose something precious.

"I can't ask you to go through what you did today again. You deserve to be able to not have to worry about things like that," I whispered.

"I'm going to stop you right there. No, let me talk," he said when I tried to speak. "You can't let them rule your life like this anymore. If you break up with me, they win. Also, I'm not so weak that a few lame moves by a couple of dickheads are going to send me running."

He approached slowly and slipped his arms around me again. I melted into him after a few moments of trying to steel myself. So much of what he said made sense and he was right, I knew that, but I couldn't help feeling that letting him stay in my life was incredibly and entirely selfish.

"Come on. We can watch a movie or something." I took him by the hand and led him into the house. Drea and the rest of them would be home eventually, but I just wanted a few minutes of the sanctuary he provided.

Mark stayed for dinner. The first time he had ever done so. As luck had it, Dad had to work late and Drea was out with friends, so it was just May and us. Oddly, I didn't find it completely unbearable. May was kind and open in ways Dad most certainly was not, and without Drea there, I didn't have to walk on as many eggshells.

I wished I could like May, especially in moments when it was just us, but I couldn't. Too much had been stolen from me because of May's very existence, and I was reminded of that even more now that her bump was becoming more and more pronounced.

Mark charmed her of course. He charmed everyone; he had that unnamable quality people like him always have. Austin had had it too.

"You should bring him around more." May smiled at me.

"Yes, she should," Mark agreed, making us both laugh.

"It's your humble nature that makes you so appealing." I poked him playfully.

After dinner, Mark and I went up to my room on the pretense of doing homework. May let us go upstairs alone without so much as a peep. Had Dad been home, we wouldn't have made it past the first stair. Assessing the situation as it was, Dad would kill Mark if he saw us now.

We were entangled on my bed. On top of the covers, but I was pretty sure if I'd invited him under, he would gladly follow. We hadn't slept together yet, but we'd been close a few times. Mark pulled back so that his lips hovered playfully over my own, a smile broad on his face.

I reached my head forward, but he pulled back further. Games like this were a favorite of his. Only when I caught him did he kiss me back. I feigned disinterest and then jolted forward, catching his head with my hands and planting my lips firmly to his. He wrapped his arms further around me and lowered down, so our bodies lined up in a perfect and frustrating way.

I felt heat spread along my body. Everywhere he touched me, my skin scorched. Moving my hands with deliberate slowness, I inched them under his shirt and began to slip it up his chest. He pulled back to allow me to fling it off over his head and caught my mouth with a new intensity. My fingertips danced against the firm muscles of his chest.

Both of us were caught up in a spell so tightly, we didn't hear the sound of Mark's phone vibrating on the bedside table until it had been going for several seconds. "Ignore it," Mark said against my lips.

Determined to do just that, I sat up to allow him access to remove my shirt. His hands grazed my ribs as his phone vibrated again.

"Just answer it and tell them to go away," I grumbled.

He groaned and disentangled himself. His brow wrinkled at the caller ID. "Hello," he said into the phone.

I couldn't make out what the person on the other line was saying, but I heard the panic in the way their voice grew louder with every passing second.

"Okay. Okay, I'm on my way." Mark ended the phone call and began moving in a frenzy. He snatched his shirt from the floor and threw it on to cover his chest. Grabbing his keys and wallet from the side table, he looked frazzled and confused.

"What is it?" I asked, trying not to panic.

"My dad called. Something happened to the store. I have to get over there." He put his belongings into his pockets without looking at me.

"Of course. I'll go with you," I said and began to inch off the bed to join him.

"No," he barked and then softened when he looked at my hurt expression. "No, I've got to go deal with this. It's nothing to worry about. Please. Stay." He leaned over and gave me a quick kiss before dashing out the door.

I went downstairs to try to convince him to let me come with him, but by the time I reached the front foyer, he was already in his car and all I could do was watch him back down the driveway.

Part of me wanted to follow him in my own car. Concern for Vincent and Mark radiated through me, but Mark had been so adamant about me staying here. As I closed the door, May came toward me with two mugs of what smelled like hot chocolate.

"Oh Candace, I was just about to bring these up to you and your *friend.*" May shot me a conspiratorial smile, like she was in on some big secret. The smile on her face was so vibrant, I almost felt sorry to shoot her down.

"That's really nice May, but he just left."

"Oh." May's face deflated. She examined the mugs like she had no idea what to do with them now.

"I'd still like a hot chocolate if that's an option," I said.

Her face brightened once more. "Of course it is! Careful, it's hot."

I gently took the mug and blew on the hot liquid before drinking it. Smooth chocolate filled my mouth. I'd had May's hot chocolate before, but it had been a while. It still tasted perfectly sweet without being overpowering. It was good, but not enough to distract me from Mark's departure.

"Thanks, May. It's really good."

I didn't think it was possible for May to look happier, but she beamed at my compliment. "It's been a long time since I made it. Drea's friends never come over anymore, and the last time I made it for just Drea, she—" May shook her head, deciding against continuing. "It's all been so hard on her."

I wanted to remind May that it had been her own actions that had made anything hard on Drea, but the look of regret on her face made me bite my tongue. Deep down, May knew she'd been wrong, and it didn't do anyone any good to remind her of it.

Instead of comforting May, which would have been far too awkward, I thanked her for the hot chocolate and retreated to my room. I did give her a slight pat on the arm as I walked by. It was all I had for her.

When I snatched my phone from my side table, I hoped to find a text from Mark, but there was only one from Mom, reminding me that she was coming home Saturday. I sent off a quick text to her. I was excited to see her, but my excitement was stifled with worry for Mark. I thought about texting him, but didn't want to bother him while he sorted out whatever had gone wrong at the bookstore.

I looked at the clock. It was just past nine. The bookstore closed at seven on select weeknights. Whatever had happened to it had happened after Vincent had gone home.

I crawled into my disheveled bed. The blanket smelled like Mark's clean shampoo, and I couldn't help but wrap myself in it.

My phone chimed some time later, pulling me from sleep. Looking at the clock, I saw that it was almost midnight. The text from Mark was shorter than I would have liked.

“Just got home. The store had a window or two broken, but don’t worry the police are looking into it. I’ll see you tomorrow. Sleep tight.”

Frustrated, I put my phone back on the nightstand. I should have been relieved that the place hadn’t burned down, but vandalism wasn’t much better. My mind raced with scenarios, hoping that by some miracle Drea and Luke weren’t involved. Then there was the bit about him telling me not to worry. Usually when people said that, it meant there was a chance that I should.

Chapter 20

What happened to the bookstore most likely wouldn't be in the morning paper, but it would definitely make the local news website. I'd gotten up earlier than I'd intended and found myself sitting at my desk, entering in the local news station web address. Mark had told me not to worry, but I couldn't shake the feeling that he hadn't told me the whole truth about what had happened.

When I found the article, I saw he had most definitely downplayed the damage. I clicked on the images with the article and found that when Mark said one or two windows, he meant all of them. Glass cracked and broken into jagged pieces was front and center. There was no information about who was responsible, but I knew.

Tears pricked my eyes, and I slammed the top of my laptop down, unable to see anymore. Shame flooded every fiber of my being. Mark didn't deserve anything being done to him. Vincent didn't deserve it. It was only because of me that it was happening at all.

Mark had convinced me yesterday that he didn't care about whatever they did to him, but I did. I couldn't be selfish and keep him when it meant he paid the price.

Drea and the rest wouldn't stop until I was alone again. I'd give them whatever they wanted if it meant they'd leave him alone.

I'd just finished getting dressed when my door opened. Drea stood in the doorway looking gleeful. "Good morning," she purred. "How's your boyfriend this morning?"

My fists clenched by my sides. "Why go after him? Your problem is with me. Take it all out on me and leave him alone."

She put on a fake pout. "Where's the fun in that?" She stood there for a moment taking in my anger, and she let out a laugh. "You did this Candace. I played nice for a while, but you just had to come out of hiding. You just had to make Luke… you know what? That doesn't matter."

She pushed off from the door and walked down the hall. When she was out of eyesight, she called, "I'm just getting started with your boyfriend."

I went over to the door and slammed it shut. I slid down until I hit the floor and curled up. She wouldn't stop. Mark would keep getting hurt. He'd resent me one day, and I would hate myself.

I only had one option. Just thinking about what I had to do made the small ache in my chest grow to a painful piercing sensation. It would hurt, but I had to make this right.

You broke it Candace, so fix it. Fix it was what I intended to do.

***

The parking lot at school was just starting to fill up when I pulled my car in. It was easy to spot Mark only a few spots away, waiting for me as he usually did. My heart stuttered at the sight of his smile, and I prayed for the strength to do what needed to be done. Drea's words pushed me forward. *I'm just getting started.*

I'd practiced my speech all morning, but when he opened my car door for me, I forgot every word. He held my hand as the door shut behind me. As I stood there, I wanted to crawl into his arms and offer every apology under the sun. Instead, I took my hand out of his.

"I saw an article on the shop this morning online. It was a lot worse than you said." I let my backpack drop between us.

He let out a deep breath and looked toward the school. "I didn't want you to get all worked up. It's not as bad as they're probably making it seem."

"Maybe, but it doesn't really matter how bad the damage was. The point is that the damage happened in the first place, because of me. I said some things yesterday to Drea, and she took it all out on you because she knows anything she does to you will hurt me. This is my fault. I can't keep watching all of this happen to you. It's not fair to you or to your father."

"It doesn't matter what you said to Drea. None of this is your fault," he said calmly, though redness crept into his neck. I took in the dark circles under his eyes. I doubted he slept well last night.

"It is," I whispered and took a deep breath before continuing. "Do you think maybe we should cool this for a while? You know, let everything settle down?" I fixed my eyes to him, so he couldn't think I was uncertain.

"No, I think that's a terrible idea actually," he said. "I want to be with you. Fuck the rest." His words were concise, but his eyes swirled with emotion.

When I said nothing, he asked, "Do you want to be with me?"

My chest constricted. I knew he asked me the question because he was so sure my answer would be yes. If I gave him the truth, I'd watch him get hurt over and over again until he hated me. Until we'd be ruined. I couldn't do that. I was in too deep with him to be selfish.

"No," I lied, taking care to keep my voice from cracking.

He opened his mouth, then closed it. He stared at me like I'd hit him, betrayed him, and maybe I had. "You're not a good liar, Candace."

No, I wasn't. My silence was telling, but I was afraid if I spoke anymore I would crack.

When he spoke again, he was quiet. "Is this what you really want?"

He was giving me a chance to fix it. To tell the truth and erase the last few minutes, so it couldn't stain the records of our love story, if that was what we had. He would let me. He wouldn't hold my fear against me.

Using the last of my voice and my confidence, I said, "Yes."

He nodded slowly as it sunk it. For a moment, I thought he would continue to try to talk me out of it. "I would have put up with whatever those assholes threw our way," he said and walked away without looking back at me.

"But you shouldn't have to," I whispered to his fading figure.

I wasn't sure when I'd given my heart to him, but I had. I knew it in the way I had to force my lungs to take in air. It was different than when Luke had left me. This one was deeper.

I stood at my car with my backpack at my feet and waited for the crowd outside of school to filter inside. The pain on Mark's face replayed in my mind, and I willed myself to keep it together. Once Drea and everyone saw we weren't together anymore, the pain would be worth it. It would mean something. That was what mattered. The pain needed to matter.

Keeping my head down, like I had when they had all first turned on me, I made my way quickly to my locker. I thought about throwing my hood up, so I could have an actual barrier between everyone else and me, but decided my turmoil would get back to Drea and hopefully, she'd call the dogs off Mark.

I tried to keep my pace quick, but the crowd around my locker didn't allow for that. Drea leaned against my locker, effectively blocking access to the books I needed. Mindy and Allison stood next to her. All three smiled, devil's smiles, as I approached. I looked around for Luke, but he was nowhere to be found. Perhaps, he was too cowardly to face me. Drea would never break windows herself; she had sent Luke to do it.

"Good morning again, Candace," Drea said. One booted foot was crossed over the other as she leaned back.

I'd known this was coming. Drea had already gloated once this morning, but she'd lacked an audience then.

"What's wrong, don't want to talk to me?" Drea pouted. Turning to Mindy and Allison, she said, "Can you believe she doesn't want to talk to us?"

Allison laughed while Mindy skulked toward me with slow, menacing footsteps. She had pinned her curls up and she wore heavy black boots; she'd come prepared for a fight. "I can, actually. She's been forgetting her place lately. Haven't you, Candace?" Mindy stopped just inches from me.

We were toe to toe. The smell of her floral perfume invaded my sinuses, making my head spin.

Red lips spread as she smiled at me. With shocking quickness, Mindy's hands shot out and caught me hard in the chest. The breath went out of me as I stumbled, but didn't fall.

"Cut it out," I said, feeling my hands ball into fists, but willed them to stay at my sides.

"She speaks!" Mindy crowed and turned to Drea.

"I thought she'd gone mute," Drea said.

"I think she thinks she's too good for us. She made a new group of friends and wants to forget us." Mindy shoved me again, this time with a bit more force. Rage coiled in my belly. "You don't get to forget us."

As Mindy reached out the third time, something inside of me snapped. A chain broke and, like a monster, I was free.

I lunged at Mindy with the entire weight of my body. Her eyes bulged in disbelief just before we went down in a clawing, punching heap. As we rolled and kicked, I didn't know which limbs were my own. It was only when I felt sharp pains that I knew Mindy landed a blow. Mindy roared as my fist connected with her eye.

Mindy still had ahold of my hair as we were suddenly ripped apart. Strong arms wrapped around my waist.

It was disorienting at first to be flung around so suddenly, but then the faces started to register. Drea's was one of them, and I couldn't contain myself as she sent me a vicious smile.

"What's *wrong* with you!" I screamed. "You won already. You took everything from me!"

Drea stepped back as I tried to dive for her, and I felt a surge of satisfaction. I had scared her. I had scared the scariest person I knew. What did that make me?

"That's enough," barked Ms. Weatherbee as she tightened her grip on my waist. It was the sharpness in her voice that made me stop struggling to break free. Ms. Weatherbee never lost her composure. "Mindy, head to the principal's office. I'll meet you there shortly. Everyone else get to class, now." Her breath came out in harsh exhales.

As everyone else scurried from the hall, Mindy looked like she wanted to argue, but thought better of it from the tone of the guidance counselor. Ms. Weatherbee was small, but the strength she held me with was of someone twice her size. Mindy righted her askew clothing and smoothed her hair before limping down the hallway. Her face looked worse than mine felt.

"If I let you go, will you attempt to attack anyone?" Ms. Weatherbee said with a scathing tone I didn't think her capable of.

"No." I shook my head, trying to get the hair in front of my face to cover the shameful tears that were already falling. Adrenaline was fading with each second and all that was left was hurt and shame.

We walked to her office in silence. The going was slow as my body felt rubbery and sore in places it shouldn't. I was directed to take a seat in Ms. Weatherbee's office while she disappeared for a few moments and reappeared with two paper towels and ice.

"Clean your self up and put the ice on your eye. It'll help with the swelling." She lifted a hand, indicating to the small mirror on the wall.

Zombie movies weren't my favorite, but I knew what the creatures looked like. As I stared at my reflection, I thought I definitely could pass for one. My eyes were puffy and glassy from crying, and one was starting to swell shut. I didn't have a split lip this time, but my nose did have a trickle of blood slowly coming out of it. I held the paper towel to my nose and the ice pack to my eye, humiliation filling me.

When I sat back down in the chair, the guidance counselor looked at me with softer eyes than moments before. "This is where I didn't want you to end up last time you were in my office," she said, looking slightly annoyed that I had failed to avoid this fate.

"I didn't think it would ever get to this point," I said, still so at a loss for how it had.

"No one ever does, but more people end up in the same position you just found yourself in than you could ever imagine." Ms. Weatherbee shook her head like she saw people banged up in her office all the time.

"I'd just had enough." Tears came to my eyes again when I remembered the white-hot rage that had filled me when Mindy had shoved me. That fight had been a long time coming, but I was still ashamed that I'd lost control.

Ms. Weatherbee rounded her desk and was at my side at an instant, every bit of instinct to help a creature in pain shining through. The soft rubbing of my shoulders only made me cry harder. Broken sobs escaped as I tried to take breaths to calm down.

A knock on the door distracted her from comforting me. Though tears blurred my vision, I recognized the intimidating form in the doorway.

"I came to see what was going on here. I've just had quite an interesting conversation with Mindy Osana," principal Whitman said, his voice strong and calm.

Ms. Weatherbee returned to her seat on the other side of the desk before explaining that she'd heard a commotion in the hallway and had found Mindy and I in a scuffle. A scuffle was putting it mildly, and I suspected she was trying to help me in some way.

"Yes, Ms. Osana explained that much to me." Mr. Whitman's eyes bore down onto mine like I was a riddle he needed to solve and fast. "Would you like to explain what happened this morning, Ms. Ellis?"

I momentarily debated not answering or saying I had no idea. It had been my way since the torture had started. Instead, I told the truth. "Mindy pushed me, and I fought back."

Mr. Whitman's lips pursed as if he were trying not to grin. "That is very similar to what Ms. Osana said, but in her version you were the aggressor."

"She's lying. She started the whole thing," I argued.

Mr. Whitman held up his hand for silence. "I'm not quite sure who started the fight, but one thing I do know is both of you were involved, which means there are consequences for both of you. You will be suspended for the remainder of the week, and I'll be notifying your parents shortly. We can't tolerate this kind of behavior here."

Suspended for the remainder of the week? I'd never even had a detention before. What about Dartmouth? Would they see that I'd been suspended and make the decision to accept or deny me solely based on that?

"Do you have anything to say or any questions?" He looked at me expectantly, like I should, in fact, have questions.

I shook my head, knowing there wasn't a thing I could say to get him to change his mind. He was known for throwing the book at students in my position.

"I've heard your name come up quite a bit this year, but I'd hoped we would never meet like this. I'm not sure what is going on, Ms. Ellis, but I suggest you pull it together."

I fought the urge to laugh. Pulling it together was what I'd been trying to do. It turned out that it was much easier said than done.

CHAPTER 21

Irresponsible. That was what Dad called me for roughly twenty minutes.

I wasn't exactly surprised to find him waiting for me when I got home. Principal Whitman had called him just like he said he would, and Dad had felt it necessary to leave work, so he could inform me how *irresponsible* I was.

I'd hoped for a bit of time to sort my thoughts before facing him, but he'd pounced on me the moment I had walked through the door.

"What were you thinking?" he boomed. He was red faced and furious. "Fighting? Have you lost your mind?"

"I was defending myself," I said, feeling my temper rise. I slid my backpack toward the stairs.

"Defending yourself? You choose to defend yourself by tackling another student? Now you're suspended and out of school. Midterms are next week. Everything you have worked for is in jeopardy." He spat slightly as he spoke; flecks of his saliva fell to the ground.

"I know that!" I shouted, surprising him. "I know what I did."

"Well, I'm glad you know now. I didn't raise you to put your hands on people!" Dad said, his voice rising to meet mine.

"No, you raised me to walk out on family."

Dad blanched and his lips thinned. "That's not fair or relevant."

"Isn't it? You think you get to yell at me now? Have some say over what I do and when I do it? You haven't been there for me since you walked out on my mom. You don't get to play the role of father now when you abandoned your post."

Dad looked at me like he didn't know who I was anymore, and really he didn't. "This conversation isn't about me and my decisions. You may hate what I've done, but you are under my roof—"

"Until Saturday," I jabbed, my anger making me bold.

"And you will follow my rules," he continued. "Consider yourself on house arrest. Get someone to cover your shifts at work. Use the time to figure out what the hell you're doing with your life. You can hate what I've done, but you're the one who decided to make irresponsible choices."

"You can't make me give up my shifts at work," I snapped.

"Actually, you're driving around in my car, so I can." He made to move into the study, like he was done with our conversation.

"And Dartmouth?" I asked hotly.

He turned back to me. "What about it?"

"Are you taking away my tuition?" I crossed my arms, ready for him to land the killing blow.

"Why would I…Is that really what all this was to you? This time that you've been here?"

"What else would it have been about, Dad? Money is how you got me here. It was always about that. It could never have been about anything else."

Dad's complexion paled. "I thought maybe we were making progress."

"How could we make progress when you're starting a whole new family?" I yelled. "You expect me to just be a smiley face in your new family portrait? It's not going to happen."

Dad opened his mouth to respond, but for a few moments no words came out. "Who are you anymore?" he said quietly.

I laughed harshly. "Don't worry about who I am. I'll be gone Saturday, and you can forget me, like you forgot Mom and Austin."

He called my name as I walked away from him, but I didn't stop. I took the stairs two at a time and didn't slow my pace until I slammed the bedroom door behind me. I called Joe and then Rachel. Both of them agreed to cover my shifts. I didn't call Mark. I was sure he would call once word got around about my fight, but my phone sat silently by me all night. He probably hated me after this morning, and maybe it was easier that way.

I crawled into bed, hoping to smell his shampoo. Even though he'd just been here yesterday, all I could smell was my own coconut body wash, like he'd never been here at all.

***

The only good thing about being suspended was that I could wallow in privacy. My plan for the week was to lie around and watch trashy television in sweatpants. In my opinion it was a solid plan. Dad took the car keys, so I couldn't go anywhere and everyone was at work, so I had free reign of the house.

On hour five of trying to figure out who really was the baby's father, I decided that maybe there was a limit to how much trash one person could watch in a day. Everyone would be home in just a few hours. School was out by now, and I was sure Drea would come home to celebrate her victory before anyone else got here.

When the doorbell rang, I felt a weary sense of hope and apprehension. I didn't know if it was Mark, but I did know I wasn't going to be strong enough to send him away. Not after everything that had happened yesterday.

When I opened the door, confusion swallowed any other emotion I felt.

"Hey," Shannon said. Her arms were full of books and papers. "I brought your assignments."

"Thanks," I said, surprised. It took me a moment to realize she was waiting to be invited inside. I stepped back and waved her in.

"How long are you out of school for?" She looked around at the tall ceilings and perfectly decorated entryway. She wrinkled her nose after a moment. "Does it always look so…white in here?"

"The remainder of the week, and yes. May likes the look of it," I said and led her into the study.

"Shit," Shannon said sympathetically.

"Yep, and on top of that I'm not allowed to leave the house. I won the jackpot."

"Seems it." We sat in silence for a few moments; the awkwardness of the situation permeated the air. "Mark filled me in on everything that happened before the fight," Shannon said quietly.

I cringed. Everyone had warned me against hurting Mark and for a moment, I wondered if Shannon had only brought my books so she would have the opportunity to say I told you so.

"I didn't want to hurt him. I just couldn't let him go through it all again and again. He doesn't deserve it." I stared at my cuticles. I couldn't look at her when I realized I'd saved Mark from the fate I'd sacrificed her to.

"No, he doesn't. Whether he wants to admit it or not, your decision was the right one."

"What?" I said, thrown.

"Drea wouldn't have stopped. Hell the only reason she left me alone was because—" Shannon stopped abruptly.

The words she didn't say hung in the air between us: Drea had left her alone because Shannon had tried to kill herself.

The opportunity for me to ask what I'd always needed to know was right in front of me. The words were wound around my tongue.

"Are you hungry?" I asked abruptly.

Shannon looked at me quizzically, but then slowly nodded.

I was moving before she gave her answer. "Great. If you still like them, I can make peanut butter and fluff sandwiches."

"I haven't had one of those in years." Shannon smiled. "Are you going to get into trouble for having me here?" She kept pace with me as I sped into the kitchen.

"No one gets home until about five thirty or so on Tuesdays, so we're safe for a few hours."

At Shannon's agreement, I made the classic sandwiches for both of us.

She watched me struggle a bit with the spreading the fluff. "Do you remember when we put that stuff in the microwave and then put it in our hair to try to give ourselves Mohawks?"

I burst out laughing. "I'd forgotten about that. My mom came in just as you'd finished gunking up my hair. I'd never seen her so mad. "

"I really thought my mom was going to have to shave my head. It took her so long to work all of it out," she laughed.

I cut her sandwich in half the triangular way, the best way, and handed it to her.

"My mom felt terrible when we walked you back home. Your dad didn't even say a word as he took you into the house."

Shannon's smiled faded. She picked at pieces of her sandwich, not really eating any of them.

If I were braver, maybe a better friend, I would have asked her about her about her sudden change in demeanor. "I'm sorry. I didn't mean to bring up a bad memory."

"No, no. It's just…I'd just forgotten about that part, that's all."

We sat in silence as we both played with our sandwiches. "Was my fight the talk of the school?"

"Yeah, actually, but it wasn't even Drea leading the charge. I heard Mindy got suspended with you. All people could talk about was how you took her down."

"They probably think I'm even worse than before," I said, biting my lip.

"No, actually. People kind of love you for it. They've wanted to knock her out for years." She shrugged.

"I snapped," I said. "It was like everything I'd kept in finally burst out."

"I told you before. There's only so much one person can take."

"Why are you doing this?" I asked suddenly.

"Doing what?"

I pushed my plate fully out of the way. "Why are you trying to make me feel better?"

Shannon looked away for a moment. She bit the inside of her cheek for a moment before looking back to me. "Because you need someone. No one should feel alone."

No one should feel alone. Yet, I'd let her feel that way for our entire freshman year. I hadn't gone to her after her suicide attempt. I wondered if I would always be reminded that she was a much better person than I was.

"I should get going," she said. "Don't want you to get caught with me here." She put her plate in the sink and walked toward the front hallway.

"You could come back," I called before I could stop myself, "tomorrow… or something." When she looked hesitant, I said, "Never mind. It was a dumb idea."

"I could do that," she said after a moment.

"Really?" I asked hopefully.

"Yeah." She nodded. "I think I'd like that."

After Shannon left, I cleaned up the kitchen. I'd never expected her to come by, but she had. It struck me that maybe if part of her had missed me, too, there was hope to fix what I'd broken between us.

***

Shannon came by after school everyday that week. We spent the time watching Netflix and reminiscing. We avoided the topic of Mark. Instead, we focused on us. On the time we'd lost. I found out she'd applied to Princeton, which is why she spent so many nights studying. We talked a little about Austin and my family's implosion, but we didn't talk about her family at all.

I never apologized for what I'd done. I wanted to, but Shannon changed the subject every time I tried. It was like she didn't need it, and she was happy where we were. We were both escaping during those few hours a day together, but from very different realities.

Chapter 22

I planned to spend the final night at Dad's vegging out. Basically, the way I'd spent my week. All I needed was popcorn and I was good to go.

Dad and May's voices were the only other noise in the house. Drea had gone to her father's again, something she had been doing more frequently since May's baby bump had become impossible to ignore.

"We can't run it over there. We're already going to be late and this dinner meeting is important," Dad said, sounding like this was a repeated argument.

"We can be thirty minutes late for dinner. She forgot it, and she needs it. She's supposed to take it nightly." May's voice was hesitant, but firm.

Their voices became muffled, but somehow louder at the same time. I reached for the remote and turned up the volume to drown out their voices. Unfortunately, I couldn't drown out the knocking on my door.

Dad appeared wearing a nice suit, looking every bit the professional businessman. "Candace, we need you to drive Drea's allergy meds to her father's apartment. She's not answering the phone, so we can't tell her to come back and get them." From his tone, it was clear this was an order, not a request.

"What's the address?" I asked, ready to put it into my phone.

My father gave no reply, and when I looked up I found him staring with his lips parted. He'd been anticipating an argument.

May, however, couldn't have looked more delighted as she rattled off the address and gave me a key to the apartment, just in case Drea and Mr. Parker weren't home.

I briefly wondered why May would have a key to her ex-husband's apartment, but I was being offered a few hours of freedom, and after being on lockdown for days, I would take what I could get.

"This one has to be refrigerated," May said, handing me a small bag of medications.

Mr. Parker lived about an hour outside of Brinkerville. Apparently, he'd bought a swanky apartment the day after May told him about the affair. Drea often made a point to bring up the fanciness of it at the dinner table, as if she had something to prove when she got home from a weekend there.

When I pulled up to the apartment, I could tell that it was far more expensive than anything my mother could afford, possibly even my father. I didn't know why any of it surprised me. Mr. Parker had always loved buying luxurious things. Exhibit A: the enormous house he'd purchased for just three people and his indifference about leaving it to his ex-wife and her lover.

After a short ride in the elevator, I was knocking lightly on the front door, hoping to drop off what I needed to and go. It occurred to me that I hadn't seen Mr. Parker since everything had happened, and I had no idea how he would take to seeing the daughter of the man who had wrecked his marriage standing at his front door.

When I stood there for a few moments and heard no movement inside, I sent up a silent thank you. I fished the key May had given me out of my pocket and let myself in. Calling out to make sure I was truly alone, I took in my surroundings.

Mr. Parker had clearly spared no expense decorating. Expensive, yet uncomfortable-looking furniture sat in the living room, and art I would never understand lined the walls. The kind where nudity was classy or something. The floor was dark and modern. Even though the place looked elegant, it felt cold.

Everything was as I had expected, with the exception of an abundance of papers and envelopes littering the main entrance table. I'd only been in Mr. Parker's office one time, but I remembered it being immaculate. The messiness in front of me made me feel like I was missing something. I looked a bit closer and realized it was all mail and flyers, some dating back to September. Why would Drea's father keep this junk, and why wasn't he reading his mail?

As I made my way to the kitchen, I noticed that the apartment gave no sign of someone living there at all. It was as if the owner had abandoned it. For some reason, the thought gave made me a shiver. It was a little creepy here.

The kitchen looked new, like no one had ever made a meal in it. It wouldn't have shocked me if Drea and her father never cooked for themselves, opting instead to dine in expensive restaurants, but I still found it all very odd. The apartment didn't look lived-in at all.

Feeling uncomfortable, I decided to find a piece of paper to leave a note for Drea, so she would know to look for her meds. It was when I was looking for paper in the kitchen drawers that I heard the front door open and close and the familiar sound of heels click against the hardwood floor. Dread filled me as I ran through the quickest way to explain my presence to Mr. Parker.

When Drea entered the kitchen, she almost dropped the bag of takeout food she held.

"What the hell are you doing here?" she demanded. Her voice had almost a desperate edge to it.

I was still waiting for Mr. Parker to come in behind her, but with every passing moment, I grew more and more certain that he wasn't coming at all.

"Your mom asked me to drop these off," I said, holding up the bag.

"Great. Get out." Drea nodded toward the exit.

I began to respond, but then I took in her outfit. She was in baggy sweatpants and Ugg boots. Never, in all the years that I'd known her, had she ever gone out looking like that. Even her hair was in a messy bun. I was sure Drea wanted me out, not because she hated me—well, maybe that was a part of it—but because I was dangerously close to figuring out something no one else had.

"Yeah, okay. I'll just put these in here."

"Don't!" Drea screamed.

But it was too late; I was already pulling the handle. The fridge was almost empty, with the exception of a few bottled waters and condiments. The mail. The fridge. Drea's attire. Wherever Mr. Parker stayed, it clearly wasn't here all that often.

"Looks pretty sparse in there," I said, shutting the door and turning toward Drea, who stood with a defiant look on her face.

"Dad's busy a lot, so we eat out." She held up the bag as if it were being put forward as evidence.

"That would explain why the kitchen looks like no one has ever used a pan on the stove," I said, growing bolder as the pieces fell into place.

"Uh, yeah. It would explain that, idiot." Drea crossed her arms.

"Is your dad so busy that he hasn't had a chance to open his mail from months ago?"

"What is this, a trial? I don't have to explain anything to you."

It was so odd to hear her like that, so close to the edge, almost broken. I thought briefly about abandoning the questioning and leaving Drea here, without ever saying the truth, even though both of us knew it.

"Drea," I said and waited for her to look at me. "Where is your father?"

Drea threw me a murderous glance, and I braced for a verbal or physical assault, as was the way when Drea was backed into a corner. But what happened next was so foreign to me that I had no idea what my next step should be.

Drea began to cry, *really* cry. Tears flooded down her face, leaving black trails of mascara and her chest heaved as sobs cracked through. She threw her hands over her face and slid down the wall until she sat on the floor. Every bit of her crumbling.

I should have done a victory dance. I'd defeated the dragon. This was the girl who had made my life hell, who had caused so much destruction, but in that moment, I saw her for what she really was: hurt and alone. I felt… sorry for her.

"I have n-no idea where he is," Drea hiccupped. The sounds she made were animalistic. Wounded. "Shit. You must love this."

"Love what?"

"Seeing me like this. Knowing everything." She took her hands from her face.

"No," I said, "I honestly don't."

Part of me wanted to walk out and leave her there with her pain, but the small bit of me, the bit that remember the girl who had held me as I'd cried over Austin, the bit that could never hate her, made leaving impossible. Slowly, I made my way over to where Drea sat and slid down beside her. I didn't touch her or try to comfort her.

"What exactly is going on?"

She bit her lip. "Dad was away all the time before, and I thought it was because of her. Then with the divorce…I realized he wanted to get away from both of us." She put the backs of her hands to her eyes, trying to clear them like a child would.

"Why do you still come here if he's not here?" I looked around, trying to understand the appeal of the place that could only be described as cold.

"At first, I was sure he'd be here. The first few times I showed up, he said he forgot when I called him. Then, he stopped answering. I didn't want anyone to kno—" She broke off and tried to take deep breaths to prevent another round of sobs. "He doesn't want me…neither of them do."

I felt her pain in my own chest. "Why not just tell May? No one would judge you for your father's actions."

"Oh really?" Drea looked at me with puffy eyes.

It took me a moment before it dawned on me that I was the perfect example of how untrue my statement was.

"I blamed you for what happened between our parents," Drea said.

"Yeah, I know. My life has been a living hell."

Drea nodded, not quite looking as ashamed as I hoped she would. "Had our parents not…Dad would still be here. Distant, but around," she said and then added, "I can't hate him, Candace."

She couldn't hate him, and she needed someone to hate. I was the perfect target.

Drea's eyes filled again, and she hugged her knees to her chest, like it could plug up the emotions leaking from her. "If I said I was sorry, would it make a difference?"

"Are you?" I whispered. "Sorry?"

She said nothing, but began to cry again in earnest. It was as if every ounce of repressed hurt poured from her. I knew a lot about hurt and pain, most of it because of the broken girl next to me. I could have condemned her, but I didn't. Instead, I wrapped my arm around her shoulder and comforted the greatest enemy I'd ever known.

CHAPTER 23

Sitting on the couch with Mom felt right. Soft throw blankets cuddled in around us. The pint of cookie dough ice cream we shared didn't hurt either.

"Ohhh, he's a stud," mom said and popped another spoonful into her mouth.

"Ew. No, he's like fifty."

We were on our second feel-good movie of the night, and had made a game of assessing the female heroines' romantic interests.

"Silver hair is the new black hair," Mom said wisely, making us both laugh.

We'd been back together since earlier that morning, and though I'd briefly wondered if our reunion would be awkward, we'd picked up without missing a beat.

Dad hadn't been home when I'd left, and in a way I was thankful. I didn't want an awkward goodbye, full of false promises to see each other. He'd left me a card in a sealed envelope, but I hadn't read it yet.

"We older folk call men like that silver foxes. You'll appreciate them when you're older."

"I doubt it. I'm off men for the foreseeable future," I said, digging deeper into the sugary coolness of the ice cream.

"Ah, I was wondering when this would come up".

"What's that supposed to mean?" I worked my words around a big piece of cookie dough.

"Before this past week, Mark was a topic you couldn't seem to help bringing up. What happened?" Mom looked at me with concerned eyes.

I sometimes found it frustrating that Mom was so good at reading me, but in that moment I couldn't have been more thankful. It was easier to talk about when someone else brought it up.

"I just don't think I'm right for him, so I broke it off," I said.

"Why on earth would you think that?"

"I don't know. It's just … it's just that he's a good person, and sometimes I feel like I'm not. Like I have all this stuff in my life that will complicate his." I knew I wasn't explaining it well at all.

"I'm not sure I know what you mean by 'stuff.'"

I shrugged and played with the soft blanket in front of me. "Things in my life blew up when Dad left. I've got so much baggage now, and I don't want him to have to carry it."

"Your father called me every now and then while you were at his house," Mom said.

"He did?" It was hard to believe Dad would ever pick up the phone to call Mom.

"Mhmm. He called to update me on how you were doing and for advice. Apparently, you didn't make it easy for him to make amends." Mom's words weren't quite an accusation, but I felt the weight of them.

"He didn't make anything easy when he left," I said as the big-breasted actress on the screen poured her heart out to the guy who didn't deserve her.

Mom's eyes shone. After a moment, she reached over and took my hand. "I think I made a mistake not stepping in to help you get past everything sooner. I was too focused on being single over forty-five." She gave me an apologetic smile.

"You didn't make a mistake. He left you, too. Anyway, when did you become an advocate for Dad?"

"When he called devastated that he didn't know how to talk to you anymore. I never meant to help create a wall between the two of you."

"He did this to himself. He's the one that fell out of love with this family."

"Oh, sweetie." Mom shook her head trying to find the right words. "You're father and I hadn't been in love for a long time when he decided to leave."

My mother's admission was one I'd thought about a few times, but always brushed off. Of course they were still in love. Things had been rough after Austin, but they were still in love.

"Your father and I discussed divorce right before Austin's accident, but then when he died, we couldn't stand tearing your world apart further, so we decided to stick it out until we thought you were ready."

"No, that doesn't make sense. You were devastated when he left." I remembered the memory like it had happened yesterday.

Mom nodded. "Yes, I was, but not because I was still in loved him. It was because he broke the promises we made, and he broke the vows we took when we first got married. I may not have loved him like I did when we were first married, but I still valued the commitment we made."

I inched toward her, feeling closer to her than I ever had. "I'm still mad at him," I said thickly.

"I know." Mom wrapped her arms around me and rocked gently. "But you can't let anything that happened between your father and me affect how you treat other people you care about. Baggage is only baggage if you decide to carry it. You do get to let it go, you know."

I nodded against her shoulder. She made sense, but letting go of my anger and other emotions was easier said than done. I'd carried my baggage for months, not a long time in the grand scheme of things, but long enough for it to feel like it was a part of me. I didn't even know how to begin getting rid of it.

Mom and I sat together, both a little teary. It was when I started to nod off a bit later that she brought me upstairs and tucked me in like she had done when I was five. Sleeping in my own bed again made me realize how much I'd missed it.

It also made me sleep heavier than I normally did. But the knocking sounds broke through eventually. I wondered how long the pounding on our front door had been going on by the time I reached it. My mother was only a few feet behind me, pulling on her robe.

Shannon fell through the doorway as I opened door. She only managed to catch herself before falling to her knees. Her red hair was frizzy and wild around her face.

"Shannon, what the—" I broke off when I took in the rest of her appearance. Her pajama pants were torn at the knee and blood stained the fabric, as if she had fallen hard. And, oh God, she was barefoot. Her feet still had bits of snow clinging to them.

I stared, horrified. My own heart picked up as her eyes darted around in panic. Instinct kicked in and I shut the door and slammed the locks closed.

My mother kneeled by Shannon and whispered gently to her. Then, very gingerly, she guided her to the couch and indicated that I should sit beside Shannon. I moved almost robotically toward her. Mom left the room for a moment and came back with socks for Shannon and an extra blanket.

"Shannon, honey, can you tell me what happened?" My mother moved to take Shannon's hands, but stopped when she saw that they were scraped and bloodied. At my mother's sharp intake of breath, Shannon tucked her hands to her sides.

The phone in the kitchen began to ring, making Shannon jump. She grabbed my mother's shoulders almost violently. "I'm not here." When my mother parted her lips to respond, Shannon pleaded, "They can't know I'm here."

There was a wildness in Shannon's eyes that frightened me. Never had I seen anyone look so desperate. So terrified.

I don't know if it was the terrified look of Shannon or the desperation in her voice, but at Shannon's pleading, Mom nodded slowly. Something had clicked in her mind that hadn't for me.

My mother's voice was clear even from the living room as she answered the phone.

"Hello?" And after a moment, "No, I'm sorry. We haven't seen her. We'll keep an eye out though." A moment after she hung up, and my mother came back into the living room. "That was your father."

Beside me, Shannon shivered.

"I can't lie to your parents forever." When Shannon didn't respond, my mother said, "I can call the police."

At this, Shannon jerked her head up. "No, please don't."

"Shannon, I'm not sure what's going on here, but I don't think there's a way for me not to." My mother looked uncomfortable, but resolved.

"No. No, you can't. Can you call my grandmother, please? She'll come and get me." Shannon's eyes begged my mother to grant her this, and after a moment my mother sighed and relented.

As my mother made the call, I stayed at my post beside Shannon. I put my hand on her elbow, which caused her to jerk slightly.

"Sorry," I whispered and removed my hand. When Shannon said nothing, I asked hesitantly, "What's going on?"

For a moment, Shannon focused on the carpeted floor of our living room and then she swung her eyes to me. I felt that if I said nothing and gave her enough time, she would reveal her secrets, but that wasn't the case. As quick as she looked at me, she directed her gaze elsewhere.

For the next hour, my mother and I sat with her in almost utter silence. We tried to get even the smallest of responses from her, but it was like she had shut down entirely.

When Shannon's grandmother arrived and my mother filled her in on what was going on, I waited for some kind of reaction from Shannon, but there was nothing. She just sat there.

"Thank you for looking after her," Shannon's grandmother said to my mother. Her voice wavered as she took in Shannon's appearance. She spread her arms for Shannon to fall into them, and after a moment Shannon got up and did just that.

It felt like only moments before they were both gone, leaving my mother and me shaken.

"You should try and get some sleep," Mom said.

"I don't think I can."

Mom put her hand on my back to guide me to the couch. She allowed me to cuddle into her as I went through everything with Shannon. Before long, I felt my eyes get heavy, and though I tried to fight it, I couldn't avoid sleep's claim on me. I hoped that when I woke, I was in my own bed, and everything with Shannon had been a dream.

***

Early this morning, a police cruiser was in the Bowen's driveway, but it appeared that they left without incident. I may or may not have known that because I watched out my window as they came and went without arresting anyone.

I was studying for midterms, or trying to, when my mother came in with an update.

"She's been moved to some sort of rehab facility," my mother said as she sat down on my bed.

"Wait, for, like, drugs?" I asked, not understanding.

"No, more so for mental health. Shannon's grandmother went there with her this morning. Apparently, Shannon isn't talking about last night, and the doctors are afraid for her stability."

I leaned forward. "She looked so afraid last night, Mom. When she got here she looked like she'd just fought someone."

"I know. I know," my mom said with her hands up. "Unfortunately, the doctors seem to think maybe it was self-inflicted."

"What?" I barked. "There's no way. Shannon wouldn't hurt herself."

"Hey, I'm only relaying information. Take it easy on me." When I muttered an apology, she continued, "History is against her, Candace."

The reminder that Shannon had once tried to take her own life wasn't necessary. It was with me all the time, but nothing had happened this time to make her take such extreme measures.

"She didn't hurt herself," I said.

I was sure Shannon hadn't had some sort of mental break. I felt it. The fear in her had been palpable, so real it had felt like my own. I was sure it was something else, and as I looked out the window toward the Bowens' house, I was sure I knew what that something—or some*one* was.

I did everything I could to keep my mind off of Shannon. I studied, cleaned, and finally unpacked the bags I'd taken to Dad's. When my hands skimmed over the card, I contemplated throwing it away, but who was I kidding, I could never not know what it said. A slip of rectangular paper fell from the card as I opened it. It took me a moment to realize what it was.

"Holy shit," I murmured. I looked back at the card and read it.

Dear Candace,

Enclosed is the money for Dartmouth or any other school you choose. It's enough to get you through your first four years. I should have offered it to you, not tried to bribe you. I only wanted you to let me back in. I'm sorry I failed you in more ways than one, but know my time with you has meant the world to me. You can't forgive me, and I understand that. I will always want you and love you.

Love,

Dad

My hands shook as I stared at the amount on the check. He'd destroyed my world, and was giving me a chance at whatever future I wanted.

I grabbed my phone. My fingers hovered above his number. After a moment, I clicked my phone off. What did the note and money really change? Something inside of me screamed that it changed everything, but I beat it back.

Chapter 24

School that Monday was oddly quiet. It was like everyone had been waiting for what was coming between Drea and me, but without saying so, a truce had been called between us that night at her father's apartment.

As I passed my old friends, none of them even so much as looked my way. Drea and I weren't ever going to be friends again, but the small debt that I owed her had been paid. I'd witnessed her broken, and I did my best to comfort her, as she had helped me years before. Now, we were even.

When I saw other members of the Top Ten in the hall, I waved hello. Did they know about Shannon? Something in their easy smiles told me they didn't. I'd asked my mother earlier that morning to find out if and when I could visit her. I still didn't know the full story, but I did know this time I wasn't going to let her go through whatever she was dealing with alone. We weren't best friends again, but she'd run to my house when she'd been afraid, and I wasn't going to let her down…again.

The only person I'd contemplated telling the events of the other night to was Mark, but I'd shut that idea down quickly. We hadn't spoken in a week. While I sat in chemistry, I wondered how it would be to see Mark for the first time. Would he hate me as Luke had when we'd broken up?

When Mark arrived, he sent me an easy smile and sat next to me. "Ready for the midterm?" My mouth dropped open a bit. "What?" he asked.

"Nothing," I replied. "I just didn't know how this was going to go."

"Oh, well as you can see I'm fine," he said.

"I'm glad," I said weakly.

I was thankful that Mr. Mason handed out the exams right after that, so we didn't have to talk anymore. It was hard enough sitting next to him, feeling a disconnect. *Fine.* It was good that he was fine. I wanted him to be fine without me, but it hurt like a motherfucker to know he actually was.

He waved to me as he left the exam. A smile in place, but it wasn't the one I was used to. It made me miss him even more.

By the time lunch rolled around, I decided I needed a break from everyone, so I opted for the library. A girl who lived on my street had apparently seen the police car in the Bowens' driveway, and rumors began to swirl when everyone realized Shannon wasn't in school today.

When the door to the quiet room banged open with a muffled apology, I cringed. Luke's form crowded the doorway before spotting me. I blinked at him in confusion before letting my face transform into a scowl. I really didn't want to deal with him today.

"I don't think I've ever been in here before," Luke said, looking around. He sat in the seat next to me after a moment.

"What do you want, Luke?" I asked tiredly, not bothering to put down my book.

"I just wanted to see if you were okay." His voice was genuine, and his eyes were soft.

"I'm fine," I said, feeling anything but.

He leaned forward. "Really?"

I let out a sigh. "Why do you care?"

"I just do," he said, sounding confused. "So are you really okay?"

I shrugged. "In some ways, yes. In some ways, no."

He nodded like he knew what I was talking about. "Anything to do with Mark?"

"You finally know his name isn't Mike?" When he glowered at me, I said, "Things aren't too good actually."

Luke chewed on the inside of his check. "I knew that," he said surprising me. Then again, everyone knew everything about everyone in our school.

"Then why did you ask?" I said, and finally put my book down.

He paused for a moment and then nodded like he was talking himself into something. "I'm the one who did that stuff to his dad's shop. Well, me and a few of the guys. I told my mom that it was me last night. We're going to the police station today."

I sat up straighter. I knew in my bones he'd done it, but I never really expected him to admit it. "Why are you telling me this?"

"Because that's not me. I don't even know what came over me. I was just so pissed that you had moved on…I don't want to be that person. I don't want you to see me as that person. I've done a lot of shit to people over the years, but I never felt bad until I saw you in the parking lot last Monday." He leaned back in his chair as if he could distance himself from his words.

Last Monday. The day I had broken up with Mark. Luke had been there somewhere. Watching.

"It's big of you to take responsibility. I'm sure Mark and his dad will appreciate it."

"I didn't do it for him," he said sadly. "Do you think the two of you will work it out?"

It was something I'd avoided asking myself. I had let him go to save him from pain. I never expected to solve my Drea problems and be free. Now that I was, Mark was on my mind a lot, but he said he was fine. Maybe I should just let him be.

"He misses you," Luke said in a sure voice. "It isn't hard to see. I felt that way once, too."

"I just saw him, and he seemed fine. Happy even," I said.

Luke laughed. "It's a show."

I stared at him. "When did you become the expert on Mark?"

"I'm not, but I know what it's like to put on a show around you. I did it for months. Trust me, he'll forgive you."

We sat in silence for a few moments before he said lowly, "I really am sorry."

"Me too," I said. In a way I was sorry. Not for my feelings now, but I was sorry for his pain. He'd been collateral damage in Drea's war.

I reached over and squeezed his hand, knowing it would be the last time. Even sitting here together felt unnatural, but he'd been the first boy I'd ever loved, and we were bound in a way because of it. It seemed almost fitting that closure with him would lead me back to Mark.

***

As I pulled into the parking lot, I gave myself the pep talk I'd come up with after talking with Luke. I'd found out from Greg that Mark had been spending his time at the bookstore, trying to fix the damage. Looking at the bookstore now, I couldn't tell any vandalism had ever taken place. The windows had been replaced and the glass had been cleaned.

Snow began to fall, and it made everything look sugar-kissed. Like I was in a fairy tale. But I wasn't a princess who needed saving, and Mark was much better than any prince.

I couldn't see inside the store, but Mark's car was in the parking lot. When I went inside, I was pleasantly surprised to see that there wasn't a lot of damage done to it. Almost everything was as I'd always known it.

It didn't take me long to find Mark. He sat on the floor wearing jeans and a black t-shirt, sifting through books. There were stacks of books circling him.

"Need any help?" I tried to keep my voice quiet so as not to startle him, but even so, he almost dropped the book he was holding.

With assessing eyes, he took me in, like he was debating whether or not I was an apparition come to haunt him. His mouth was in a hard line at first, but a careful mask of politeness took over. "Sure, that'd be great."

I knelt down next to him, taking care to not knock the stacks over. I picked up a book with the pages stuck together.

"These were the books closest to the windows," Mark explained. "I've been sorting through them since the start of the weekend. These piles are salvageable. Those aren't." He indicated to both piles, so I could follow his lead.

"How many did you lose?" I asked, feeling sorrow for the ruined stories.

"A fair amount. Dad's at home sorting through new boxes to see if we have any replacements."

"I'm really sorry, Mark." I felt like I'd said the phrase hundreds of times, but it was all I had. Nothing else seemed to fit.

His mouth quirked up on one side. "You keep apologizing for other people's bullshit."

"I'm working on that."

"My dad texted before you got here. Apparently, someone confessed to the vandalism."

"Luke said he was going to," I said, happy he followed through.

"You talked to him?" he asked, notes of slight jealously in his voice. "He's probably loving you breaking up with me."

I could work with his jealousy, if it meant I had a chance at fixing things. "No, actually," I said. "He knows where my heart is."

He sat staring at the book in his hands for a moment. "And where is that?" His mask of false happiness slipped. His eyes were hard as they looked at me, but his voice was soft, like he was reaching for a lifeline.

Before I could debate it, I gently took the book from his hands and laid it beside him. He held his breath as I moved around him. There was a familiar want in his eyes that made me brave enough close the distance between us.

But just before our lips touched, Mark put his hands on my shoulders. "What happens if things get rough again?"

"Then we deal with it together."

"How do I know you won't leave me again?"

"You don't. You'll have to trust my word," I said, hopeful that a piece of him still did.

He contemplated me for a moment. His dark eyes searching mine before he lowered his head. The moment our lips touched, Mark's hands were on me, searching, memorizing. He let out a relieved groan as his lips moved against mine. I'd missed the softness of his lips, the way his body felt against mine.

He released me briefly to shove the books near us aside before pulling me to him and soon under him. We kissed and moved against each other like we had been separated for years and not just days. As I kissed him, I felt like something I'd lost, had been found.

When I pulled back, he brought his forehead to mine. It took me a moment to catch my breath. "I was wondering how long you were going to be stubborn," he said and smiled, leaning forward to close the distance one more. He enveloped me, but didn't overtake me. It was always that way with him. There was a beauty in it.

"One week was hard enough," I said, and brought my lips to his once again.

CHAPTER 25

The facility's bright tones combated the greyness of winter enough that it looked welcoming, but I was still hesitant to go inside. Perhaps I'd seen *One Flew Over the Cuckoo's Nest* one too many times. The twinkle lights lining a couple of plants in the lobby did little to make me feel comfortable. It was probably an attempt to decorate for the holidays, which were only a few days away.

Shannon had reached out a few days after she'd been admitted. It had been in that phone call that she'd given me permission to give Mark only the necessary details of her absence. It had also been in that phone call that I'd begged her to let me see her. She'd been reluctant at first, but eventually she'd relented.

I'd debated asking Mark to drive me, but I knew this was something I had to do on my own. The rehab facility was different than I'd imagined. There were no mumbling people shuffling down the halls and no wicked nurses (that I saw). When a kind looking nurse led me to the visiting room, I found Shannon sitting alone.

The room was brighter than I'd pictured it. There were a few plants near the windows. These ones lacked twinkle lights. For the most part, it was pretty sparse, but not altogether uncomfortable.

Part of me expected to find a disheveled, wrecked teenage girl sitting there, but Shannon looked put-together; healthy even. It was a stark contrast to the terrified girl who had almost broken down my door.

"Hey," I said as I took a seat across from her.

"Hey, how's the outside world?" Her smile was guarded. At least we weren't going to avoid that she for all intense and purposes *was* as isolated from the outside as she could be.

"You're not missing anything," I said.

"I'm not sure whether that's sad or great," she said thoughtfully. She pushed up the sleeves of the long shirt she wore.

Her hands had mostly healed, but were still pinkish and raw-looking in some places.

"You look good."

"Come back a little later. They start electrotherapy at four," she said.

I felt my mouth drop open slightly, but recovered when Shannon rolled her eyes. "So how is it here?" I hadn't seen much of it, but it seemed pretty okay, you know, for what it was.

"I can't complain. They feed me, and I have my own room, but I have therapy everyday, and I'm not one to talk about my feelings. The therapist's okay though. She doesn't push me."

I wondered how useful therapy was if she wasn't sharing anything. "Feelings can be tough," I agreed. "How long do you have to stay here?"

"They offered to release me already, but I wasn't sure…" Her eyes darkened for a moment as if the thought of leaving were deeply unpleasant.

"Why would you want to stay?" I didn't mean offense by it, but I didn't see the appeal of this place.

She nodded toward the window. "Out there, people want answers that I'm not ready to give."

"Are there any answers?" I asked, quietly.

Shannon stared at me like she didn't know whether I was friend or foe. "There are always answers. Sometimes I just don't want to give them."

Her voice sounded so far off, like she wasn't really here with me. Like her body was here, but her soul wasn't.

"Are you still not speaking to your father?" Shannon asked. The question caught me off guard.

"No, I'm not," I admitted, though I'd pulled his contact information up on my phone on more than one occasion.

"You should try to work things out. Not to downplay your situation, but he loves you, and it could always be worse."

I wondered momentarily what worse was. "What happened on Sunday?"

Instead of telling me to go to hell, she said, "I didn't get into Princeton. I applied early action. I got the letter Saturday."

It was such a strange admission that I didn't follow her. "I don't understand—"

"It's where *he* went. The only school he'd pay for. I told you before that I needed to get away from this place." She looked at me with her haunted eyes.

The gravity of her words settled in. Mr. Bowen, the tense man, the man with the darkness. She was afraid of him.

"They think I hurt myself."

"*I* don't," I said vehemently.

She wrinkled her nose. "They think because I did it before, it's the same now."

"They're wrong." I don't know what possessed me, but I took Shannon's hands in mine. It felt awkward at first to reach across the table, and she barely registered I was touching her. "I wasn't there for you. I let you down. It may not be enough, but I'm here now."

She didn't speak. She didn't look at me. It was like she was trying to be anywhere else, but here. "You came to me. You were afraid." I hoped giving her the place to start would trigger her back to me.

She bit her lip as her eyes glistened. "I don't know what I was thinking. I needed help, and I knew you were there."

"You can trust me."

"Like before?" The hollowness in her voice made my heart ache.

"No," I whispered. "Not like before. I'll never forgive myself for being the reason or a part of the reason you wanted to die."

Shannon looked at me with a startled expression. Her eyes roamed my face for a moment. "You weren't the reason, Candace. What happened was awful. You were awful, but you weren't the reason. You and Drea were terrible, but you were nothing compared…I just, I didn't want to be *his* anymore."

She took a steadying breath. Even though I'd just told her I would listen, part of me want to block my ears. Whatever was coming would tear so much apart the moment she spoke, but I needed to be here to hear her truth. I needed to be the person she'd trusted before. I needed to bear witness.

"My father…" She stopped and swallowed some of her emotion back. "I wasn't sick when I was younger. It was his excuse… to keep me home. It started when I was five."

As Shannon described how her father had done to her the worst things a father could do, I held her hand, providing her strength when she faltered or struggled for words. When she cried, I didn't look away or pretend she wasn't. She was entitled to her hurt and betrayal. When she reached the end, her tears fell with an ease that scared me, like a lifetime of devastation had finally broken free.

"I'm going to tell them," Shannon said. "My doctors. I'm not sure what happens after that, but I can't survive with him. Not anymore."

"I'll be here whenever you need me," I assured her. She gripped my hand and gave me a small, broken smile. She'd been through hell, and now she had to find her way out.

I stayed with her until visiting hours were over. As Shannon and I hugged goodbye, all of me wanted to fight the coming battle for her, but if I'd learned anything in these last months, it was that we each had to fix our own brokenness. The only thing we could do was support each other. Support our fellow broken girls.

Chapter 26

I didn't know where I was going until I pulled in the driveway. His car was parked in the open garage. This moment had played through my mind since the day he'd left, but I'd always imagined he would be the one knocking at my door, asking for *my* forgiveness.

I'd said awful things. He'd done awful things. I didn't know if we could ever be the same ever again, but I would never know unless I tried. Really tried.

With a hesitant hand, I knocked softly on the door. Dad opened it a few moments later, surprise flowing into his face, quickly replaced with something like happiness.

I placed the check he'd written me in his hand. "I think I'm ready to try," I said, "if you are."

A Letter From the Author

To all the broken girls,

This book wasn't easy to write. There were a lot of parts that were painful to put on paper, but I felt compelled to tell the story. I felt so strongly for each of the broken girls in this book, and even when they are at their worst, I rooted for each of them. I hope you did too.

The world, in its current state, isn't doing girls any favors. It pits us against each other, makes life a competition, and says we can't trust each other. This isn't the case. We should be supporting each other, not tearing each other apart. The world breaks girls enough. We don't need to help break each other.

If you're a broken girl and you've identified with any girl in this book, I hope you know that you're not alone. It's okay to be broken, and it's okay to make amends.

All my love,

J. M. Ryan

Made in the USA
Middletown, DE
15 August 2017